HEAD HUNTER

HEAD HUNTER

Eric Howling

James Lorimer & Company Ltd., Publishers
Toronto

James Lorimer & Company Ltd., Publishers acknowledges the support
of the Ontario Arts Council. We acknowledge the support of the Canada
Council for the Arts which last year invested $24.3 million in writing
and publishing throughout Canada. We acknowledge the Government of
Ontario through the Ontario Media Development Corporation's Ontario
Book Initiative.

Cover design: Meredith Bangay
Cover image: iStock

Library and Archives Canada Cataloguing in Publication

Howling, Eric, 1956-, author
      Head hunter / Eric Howling.

(Sports stories)
Issued in print and electronic formats.
ISBN 978-1-4594-0967-5 (paperback).--ISBN 978-1-4594-0969-9 (epub)

      I. Title. II. Series: Sports stories (Toronto, Ont.)

PS8615.O9485H43 2015   jC813'.6   C2015-903539-2
                                                C2015-903540-6

James Lorimer &	Canadian edition	American edition
Company Ltd., Publishers	(978-1-4594-0967-5)	(978-1-4594-0968-2)
317 Adelaide Street West,	distributed by:	distributed by:
Suite 1002	Formac Lorimer Books	Lerner Publishing Group
Toronto, ON, Canada	5502 Atlantic Street	1251 Washington Ave N
M5V 1P9	Halifax, NS, Canada	Minneapolis, MN, USA
www.lorimer.ca	B3H 1G4	55401

Printed and bound in Canada.
Manufactured by Friesens Corporation in Altona, Manitoba, Canada in
August 2015
Job #215809

For Alison, Willy, and Mikal

CONTENTS

1 SLAMMING DOORS

Colt Taylor's stomach growled.

Playing middle linebacker for the Woodside High Warriors junior football team took a lot of energy. He always had a gigantic appetite after practice. Now he was ready to wolf down his dinner.

"What's on the menu, Mom? Italian? Mexican? Chinese?"

"Something closer to home. We're having good old mac 'n' cheese," she said, placing a huge, steaming plate in front of him.

"That sounds a lot better than lunch," he joked.

"What? You didn't enjoy that special treat I put in your bag?"

"Just because you work in the deli at Sobeys doesn't mean you have to sneak in some new mystery meat."

"I thought you might like liverwurst."

Colt winced. "I don't think anything starting with 'liver' could be good. And after taking one bite, I was right. It was gross."

"Okay, okay, I'll stick with ham or roast beef." Colt's mother laughed.

"When's Coach getting home?" Colt asked. His father was a gym teacher at Woodside. He was also the Warriors' football coach.

"He called from school a few minutes ago to say he'd be late. He sounded like he was in one of his moods."

"Some days I wonder why he gave up playing pro ball and became a high school coach. He doesn't always seem to like it."

His mom's face turned serious. "That's something you better ask him."

"I'd rather not."

"Was he losing his temper at practice again?"

"Yeah, he was chewing out the players. Telling everyone they were no good. Me included."

"That's not the way your father used to coach," she said, shaking her head.

"That's not the way he used to do a lot of things."

Colt and his dad used to throw the football around in the backyard and go to Edmonton Eskimos' games, eating hot dogs and cheering at the top of their lungs. On the way home they'd stop for milkshakes, then watch a movie and eat popcorn that same night. They were all things that didn't cost a lot of money. But they didn't have to. They were fun because they did them together.

Dinnertime used to be different, too. There was nothing Colt liked more than listening to his dad give the play-by-play of the last Warriors game. Colt would eat it up. Those were the years before he was on the team. Back when the Warriors lost more than they won. Sometimes the defeats would frustrate his dad because he was so used to winning when he'd played pro. He used to understand that the team was trying its best, though. He'd always laugh off a bad play or a loss.

But something had changed this season. He didn't care much about being Dad. He just cared about being Coach. And Coach wasn't laughing.

The door from the garage closed. Coach walked into the kitchen and sat down. He flashed a rare smile. "Something smells good."

"I thought you'd like it," said Colt's mom.

"So, what's on tap for tonight?" Coach asked, looking around the table.

"I've got a good book I'm reading."

"And I'm going over to Andrea's house," Colt said. "I already did my homework at school so I'd have time."

"So, I'm left all alone?" Coach said, narrowing his eyes. "Typical."

"How about some tasty apple crumble to finish up, Colt?"

"Not tonight, Mom. Thanks," he said, pushing his chair back from the table.

"Well, then, you're excused."

"Not so fast," Coach said, thumping the table with his big hands. "Where do you think you're going?"

"To Andrea's house."

"On a school night?" he asked, raising his eyebrows. "I don't think so."

"Why not?" Colt said, his voice starting to rise.

"Shouldn't you be doing homework?"

"I just told you, I finished it all. Weren't you even listening?"

Coach pursed his lips in frustration. "Then do some more," he said gruffly. "Your report card isn't perfect yet."

Colt's mom gave a weak smile. "He's getting good grades, Sam. He can't do homework all the time. He needs a break. And Andrea is such a nice girl."

Coach sat back and crossed his thick arms. "I don't know about her. She's taking the 'Andrea Wong, news reporter' thing way too seriously. She asks too many questions. Really gets under my skin. I'm not sure she's right for Colt. I don't think he should see her anymore."

Colt exploded out of his chair. "You can't tell me who to see. I'm fifteen. I can do what I want!"

He stomped down the hall to his bedroom and slammed the door behind him. He lay on the bed. His heart pounded. His fists were clenched. He stared at the walls of the small room trying to calm down.

Posters of his favourite linebackers looked back at him. J.C. Sherritt from the Eskimos. Jerod Mayo from the New England Patriots. Clay Matthews from the Green Bay Packers. And one more. An all-star linebacker wearing a famous black uniform from an earlier time. Number fifty-five from the Pittsburgh Steelers. A menacing shot of him flying through the air about to tackle a quarterback head-first. The poster was even autographed by the player — Sam "The Slam" Taylor. Colt was sick of fifty-five staring down at him. He leaped from his bed and ripped down the life-size picture of his father.

Colt was tired of always being told what to do. He knew he had to take orders from Coach on the field. That's the way football was. *But at home, too?* He wished he could shut his father up. Block out his voice. But even now he could hear him down the hall. The kitchen was so close he couldn't escape listening to more of his parent's conversation.

"You've got to control your temper, Sam. Let Colt go to Andrea's."

"He's not going anywhere. And that's final."

Colt knew his mom was on his side, but even she gave up. There was no point arguing when his father was in such a bad mood.

"Why don't we relax and watch TV for a while?" she suggested.

"One of those sappy doctor shows you like? Forget it. They give me a headache. Which reminds me, where did you hide that bottle of Tylenol? I keep forgetting where you've put it."

"In the bathroom cabinet where it always is."

"I'm going to take a couple."

"You've been taking a lot lately," Colt's mom said. "Your headaches seem to be getting worse and worse."

"I can handle it," Coach grumbled.

"Are you sure you don't want me to make you a doctor's appointment?"

"No, it's a pain I can deal with. Just like my son."

2 STORM WARNING

The Warriors were in a battle.

The Highland Hurricanes had already stormed down the field for two touchdowns. They flooded like a tidal wave into Warrior territory, leaving a path of first-down destruction in their wake. Now they were threatening to strike again.

The Hurricanes' quarterback was tall, strong, and had a passing arm like a gun. He had masterminded every play of the drive. The Warriors had no answer for the rampaging runs and pinpoint passes. Travis Valiant, number twelve in the red uniform, had to be stopped. And Colt knew it.

Colt wasn't just the Warriors' middle linebacker. He was also the captain and heart of the defence. He was the player Coach Taylor depended on to bring every running play to a grinding halt. He was the stopper. Some of his teammates might have been bigger, but none were stronger. Colt raised his hand and called for a defensive huddle.

"Let's bring it in!"

The rest of the Warriors gathered around him. The players were black and blue — and not just because those were their team's colours. Legs were battered. Arms were bruised. Blood trickled from their bandaged fingers. The Hurricanes had pounded them right from the opening kickoff. Now there was under a minute left in the first half. The ball was on the Warriors' twenty-yard line. The Hurricanes wanted to thunder across the goal line again.

Billy "Bulldog" Baker and Greg "Gunner" Nelson dragged their tired bodies back to the huddle. As the other two members of the Warriors' linebacker squad, they formed a formidable defence.

Bulldog had been Colt's best friend since elementary school. He was short and stocky with black hair and brown eyes the same colour as his skin. Every time he made a tackle he snarled. That was how he'd gotten his nickname. Gunner was the new kid at Woodside. He was an army brat whose family moved to a new military base every year or two. He was tall and had ripped muscles from the hours he spent pumping iron in the weight room. He had a blond brush cut and steely blue eyes that never showed fear.

"This is where it ends," Colt barked. "Right here. Right now. They don't get one more yard!"

The Warriors clapped their hands and trudged to the line of scrimmage. Colt dug his cleats into the shredded turf. His legs flexed. His hands tensed. His eyes zeroed in on the Hurricanes' quarterback. Everyone expected Travis Valiant to pass.

The tall Hurricane pivot shouted out his signals. "Blue . . . twenty-five . . . hut . . . hut!" He grabbed the snap and dropped back a few steps.

Bulldog and Gunner bolted across the line to sack him before he could pass. But Colt sensed something was wrong. He realized Travis wasn't going to throw.

The Hurricane quarterback pump-faked a pass and handed the ball off to his waiting halfback. Colt had read the play perfectly. Now he had to bring down the ball carrier.

Colt closed in on his prey. But like a cheetah in full flight, the red-shirted speedster raced past him. Now Colt was the hunter. He chased down the halfback and lunged for his legs. Colt had him in his grasp, but the ball carrier was too strong. The Hurricanes' player broke free and dashed ten more yards before Sanjay and Jamal could stop him. The two Warrior safeties had dashed up from their positions in the end zone to make the tackle.

The referee blew his whistle and pointed down field. "First down!"

Colt slowly got to his feet. He was angry with himself. He shouldn't have missed the tackle. Giving up the first down was bad. But not as bad as what he knew was about to happen next.

"Timeout!" Coach shouted.

Colt trotted across the field to the Warriors' bench where Coach stood waiting. He was built like a refrigerator. The blue Warriors' windbreaker barely fit over his square shoulders. His face was tense. His jaw clenched. Fiery eyes bulged from his head like he was ready to explode. "That was the worst tackle you've made all year!" he spat.

"Sorry, Coach."

"You're supposed to be the captain."

"I know, Coach."

"The guy who stops the other team. Not the guy who lets them rush for a first down."

"It won't happen again, Coach."

"You got that right. And I'll tell you why." Coach pointed a meaty finger right in Colt's facemask. "On the next play you're going to hit that quarterback at the knees. Take him right out."

Did he hear Coach right? Did he really say to hit him dirty?

"We're going to win this game just like we've won the first four games of the season. And we're going to win the league championship, too. Nothing's going to stop us from going all the way. You hear me?"

Colt bit his lip. He wanted to say something. To disagree with Coach's orders. He knew if he smashed his big shoulder pads into the quarterback's knees it could injure the Hurricanes' player. That wasn't in Colt's playbook. He played tough and he played fair. But he knew better than to disobey his father. Especially when he was in a rage like he was now.

"Whatever you say, Coach."

"That's more like it," he said, pushing Colt onto the field.

Colt ran back to the huddle and took Bulldog and Gunner aside. "Coach wants us to take out the quarterback. Hit him at the knees."

"What?" Bulldog said, his jaw dropping. "I'll hit him hard, but I'm not hitting him dirty."

Gunner's mouth widened into a sly grin. "I've got no problem with it. I'll cut him down."

Colt didn't know what to do. Did he agree with Bulldog or Gunner? He didn't want to hurt another player, but Coach had given his orders. If he didn't follow them he'd pay the price. He'd be benched at the game. And who knew what would happen at home?

The clock was ticking. Colt didn't have time to think. The next play was starting.

The Hurricane quarterback grabbed the pigskin and scrambled a few steps back into the pocket. It was a pass play! Colt, Bulldog, and Gunner blasted across the line. The quarterback froze like a deer caught in the headlights of a car. He didn't know which way to turn. Colt and Bulldog were coming at him from the left. Gunner was barrelling in from the right. Two seconds later there was a thunderous crash. Colt and Bulldog smashed him high, while Gunner submarined him low at the knees. The ball popped loose as Travis Valiant crumpled to the ground.

Gunner pounced on the pigskin. It was Warriors' ball! He sprang up from the turf and high-fived Bulldog. He was pumped after grabbing the fumble. He reached out to Colt for a fist-bump. But Colt wasn't proud of the hit and walked right by him.

The Hurricane quarterback lay twisted on the grass. He was holding his knee and groaning in pain. Colt watched two linemen act as crutches and help him limp off.

The Warriors' defence whooped as they charged off the field. They had recovered the fumble and stopped the Hurricanes' drive. They waited to be mobbed on the sidelines.

"Colt . . . Bulldog . . . Gunner . . . get over here!" Coach shouted. "What was that stunt?"

After seeing the injured quarterback, Colt thought Coach might feel bad about ordering the hit.

"What do you mean, Coach?" Gunner asked, still grinning. "We got his knees just like you said."

Coach narrowed his eyes. "No Gunner, only *you* got his knees. These other two sissies didn't follow orders and hit him high, right in the numbers."

"But . . ." Colt began.

"But nothing," Coach said, cutting him off. "If that happens again both you and Bulldog will be benched."

Colt wondered why Coach was being so rough on

them this season. He'd yell after an interception, finger-point after a missed tackle, and kick the ground after losing a fumble. He'd even blow up if a player didn't have his jersey tucked in. Colt didn't know if Coach was mad at the whole team or just him.

Coach stood thick as a bull and glared at Colt. "I expected more from you. You're letting me down. You're letting the team down. Maybe you shouldn't be captain."

"Maybe I shouldn't," Colt said, glaring right back at his father. "But that's your call, Coach."

3 NOTHING TO REPORT

"That's what I'm talkin' about!" Gunner shouted.

The outside linebacker was still stoked about his knee-crunching hit on the Hurricanes' quarterback — a hit that launched the Warriors to a thrilling 28-21 comeback win.

In the second half Keegan, the Warriors' quarterback, had led the team to three touchdowns. He had thrown for two scores and handed off the ball to their running back for a final touchdown late in the fourth quarter. That had sealed the deal.

Colt was relieved the Warriors had pulled out the victory. He didn't know exactly how Coach would have reacted if they had lost. But he knew it would have been ugly. And he was sure that somehow he would have been blamed. The team was still undefeated just like Coach wanted. Now it was time to get the party started in the locker room.

Celebrations were breaking out faster than a bad case of zits before a big date. Bulldog and Gunner were high-fiving by their lockers. The Warriors' four-man defensive line was lip-synching to a rap tune blasting from someone's iPod. Sanjay and Jamal were ribbing Keegan about him acting in the school play. The quarterback wasn't just the leading man on the Warriors' offence. He was also the leading man in the class play, *Romeo and Juliet*.

Helmets and shoulder pads were being taken off. Hoodies and jeans were being put on. A few of the players grabbed showers while others wore sweat and dirt from the game like a badge of honour. Guys were laughing and joking everywhere. It was a great party. Except for one thing — there wasn't a girl in sight. But Colt could hear a female voice.

The reporter from the *Woodside Weekly* school newspaper was at the door. Colt sat nearby and watched her trying to get in. The only thing blocking her was Coach's hulking frame. "There are no women allowed in the men's locker room, Andrea," he said. "You know the rule."

"Well, it's a stupid rule!" Andrea shot back. "How do you expect me to write a story about the game if I can't interview the players?" Her brown eyes flashed as she poked her head around Coach, trying to see in.

Coach held up the palms of his big hands. "That's the way it was when I played pro and that's the way it is now."

"What century was that?" Andrea demanded, tossing

back her long black hair. "Women reporters have been allowed in men's dressing rooms after games for years."

Andrea Wong may have been short, but she was standing right up to Coach. She was dishing out just as good as she was getting. Colt hid a grin, not wanting Coach to see.

"You'll have to wait to interview the players," Coach said. "They're still getting changed."

The girl raised her eyebrows. "Then can I interview *you* right now?" She reached into her bag and pulled out her pen and notepad.

"I'd prefer you talk to me later in the coach's office like usual. Since we won I'll answer one question now."

Colt thought Andrea might ask Coach about the big comeback. Or about the three touchdowns the Warriors scored in the second half to win the game. He definitely didn't expect what he heard next.

"How do you feel about the injury to the Hurricanes' star quarterback?" Andrea asked.

"It was an unfortunate accident."

"So, you didn't order the hit to knock him out of the game?"

Coach shrugged. "It was just a knee injury. Happens all the time. Football is a tough sport and sometimes players get hurt."

Andrea wasn't buying Coach's story. "Yeah, right. Three guys nailing the quarterback at the same time looked like a real accident."

Colt watched Coach's shoulders tense. He was no longer in a good mood. "This interview is over," he said, shutting the door in Andrea's face.

* * *

"I don't think Coach appreciated my question," Andrea said. She slid into the red booth beside Colt at the pizza place they went to after games.

"You knew he wouldn't, Andy. Why didn't you just stick to the facts about the game?"

Colt liked how brave Andrea was, but sometimes wondered if she took things too far. There was no way Coach was going to answer her questions about the hit. Even still, Colt admired her persistence. It was a quality he'd liked from the first time they met. She had interviewed him after a game in the previous season. At first Andrea had only asked questions about the game. Then she'd started asking questions about Colt — what music and games he liked, his favourite food, and favourite class at school. Then she'd asked whether he had a girlfriend. He tried to put her off, but she wouldn't stop asking until he answered that he didn't. They had been dating ever since.

"Anyone can report on a football game," Andrea said. "So-and-so scored a touchdown. Blankety-blank made an interception. The final score was such-and-such."

"So why didn't you?" Colt said, wrinkling his brow.

"Coach would have answered those questions."

"I want to dig deeper. Get the story behind the story." She stabbed the air with her finger to make her point. "I'm working on a series of articles about players getting hurt in high school football. More and more guys are going down with knee and shoulder injuries. And there are even worse problems. Some players are getting their heads hit and suffering concussions."

Colt knew players were getting hurt, but he didn't want to discuss it. He had told Andrea he had his reasons, but not what they were. The main reason was Coach. If he found out Colt had told Andrea about the hit, he'd erupt like a volcano again. He'd probably bench Colt so he couldn't play. And then ground him so he couldn't see Andrea. He couldn't have a school reporter getting close to the truth about who ordered the takedown. Even if that reporter was his girlfriend.

"So are you going to give me the inside scoop on how the Hurricanes' quarterback got injured?"

Colt shook his head. "It was just like Coach said."

"Right . . . an accident," Andrea said, rolling her eyes. "Well, if that's the case it sure looked like Gunner, Bulldog, and you had a lot to do with causing it."

4 WHO WANTS TO WIN?

"Hide your food, my good fellows," Keegan joked in his best Romeo voice. "A most brutish knave approaches!"

Bulldog had rolled into the cafeteria and was checking out the table where the football team always sat. He looked hungry. Sanjay and Jamal slid wide apart to make room. Bulldog plopped down. His stocky frame was so wide the butt of his jeans hung over the edge of the bench.

"Are you sure you've got enough food on that tray?" Gunner asked, eyeing the stack of burgers and fries.

"Hey, this body is in top physical condition, bro," Bulldog said, patting his round belly. "And, just for the record, I'm not fat, just big-boned."

Colt smiled at Bulldog's good nature. He played tough as nails during games, but kept the team loose off the field.

"I've heard rumours about practice today," Sanjay said. "Any of you dudes know the scoop?"

Jamal nodded. "I think Coach has something up his sleeve."

"Maybe a trick play we can pull at the end of a game," Gunner said, wiping a mustard smear leftover from his third hot dog. "Whatever it is, I'm all for it if it helps us win."

Colt's teammates leaned across the table to face him. Bulldog asked what was on everyone's mind. "Shouldn't you know what's going on?"

"He is your dad, after all," Sanjay said.

Gunner narrowed his eyes. "Yeah, the captain should know this kind of stuff."

Colt shrugged. "I only know what you guys know. He may be my dad, but lately he only acts like he's my coach. He doesn't talk much about the team. And when he does, I'm just another player to him. He just gives me orders. 'Take out the garbage. Wash the dishes. Do your homework.'"

"And what if you forget to do that stuff?" Bulldog asked.

"Then I get grounded."

Bulldog shook his head in sympathy. "That's brutal, bro."

Gunner wasn't so concerned. "Yeah, yeah, we get it. Coach's little boy has problems at home. Whatever. In my house I never get to even see my dad. He's in the army and is always off fighting a war or helping poor people in Africa. So, don't give me that sob story about your life at home. At least you know your father is alive."

"All I know," Colt said, ignoring Gunner, "is that Coach wants the practice in the gym, not on the field. Beyond that, it's a mystery."

"A mystery we'll solve at four o'clock this afternoon," Gunner said, slyly as though he knew something the others didn't. "And I can't wait."

* * *

There was a white sheet of paper on the gym door. Big black letters spelled out: WARRIORS FOOTBALL MEETING — PLAYERS ONLY. Colt, Bulldog, and Gunner cruised in and joined Keegan, Sanjay, Jamal, and the rest of the team. Most of the players wore their black and blue team jackets with the Warriors' crest on the front. They stood in a large huddle at centre court, joking around while they waited. Their voices echoed through the gym like it was a cave.

Along one wall of the gym was a series of small offices. A door opened and Coach Taylor marched out.

"All right, listen up."

Conversation stopped dead. All eyes were on Coach, who now stood in front of them. His legs were spread wide. His hands were on his hips.

"I discovered something last game. I learned that we have two kinds of players on this team. I don't mean strong players and weak players. I don't care about that. What I care about are players who don't follow my orders. Players that don't do what I say. Players who won't do anything to win."

Gunner punched the air with his fist. "You tell 'em, Coach!"

"Now, I've got a simple solution to fix this problem." Coach walked in front of his army like he was inspecting a row of troops. "If you disobey me you'll be benched. It's that simple. You'll be riding the pine until your backside gets splinters. Do you hear me?"

Gunner led some of the players shouting back. "Yes, Coach!"

"I can't hear you."

"Yes, Coach!" shouted most of the players. The response was loud, but not loud enough. Coach still wasn't satisfied.

"I see some of you couldn't open your mouths." He narrowed his eyes and scanned the faces. "Let's find out who'll be first to disobey me."

The gym was deathly quiet.

"I want everyone who agrees to follow my orders to form a line over there." Coach pointed to his right.

Gunner was the first to make a move. "I'm with you, Coach!"

Soon Keegan, Jamal, Sanjay and almost every other Warrior took a few steps and formed a long line. Colt knew all those players wanted to win. So did he. But he also knew they hadn't secretly been told to take out the Hurricanes' quarterback.

"And now I want everyone who won't follow my orders to stand over there." Coach pointed to his left.

Colt stood his ground. So did Bulldog. They were the only two players who hadn't moved. Colt didn't know what to do. He didn't believe in hurting other players just to win. But he knew the consequences as well. The other players wouldn't understand. They'd think the captain didn't want to win. And worse — he'd be benched by his own father.

"I see we have a couple of rebels," Coach said. "A couple of guys who aren't willing to follow my orders." He crossed his thick arms and glared at Colt and Bulldog. "I'm going to give you one last chance. One final offer to do the right thing and join your team. A team that will do whatever it takes to win the championship."

Colt shot a glance at Bulldog and nodded. They had no choice. Coach had all the power. The two holdouts shuffled silently to the end of the long line.

5 HEADLINE NEWS

Every Friday night the Warriors got together for chicken wings. It was a tradition.

Colt and Bulldog sat at one table. Gunner, Keegan, Sanjay, and Jamal sat a few rows over shooting nasty glances back at them. Bad blood remained after the showdown in the gym. Gunner and a few other players still weren't convinced Colt and Bulldog wanted to win enough to do anything.

Colt wished Andrea was there. She often came to wing nights to interview the players for her next newspaper story. But she said she couldn't go that night. She was working on a top-secret project.

The restaurant was rocking though. Music pounded from the speakers. The place was packed with high school and college students. Everyone wanted to celebrate the end of another school week. No more math or science classes for the whole weekend! Servers sped by carrying big plates of chicken wings. Colt ate there so often he could pick out the smell of every sauce that wafted by — Spicy BBQ, Teriyaki, Honey Garlic . . . His mouth watered like a hungry dog's.

"I can't wait to order," Bulldog said. His sausage-like fingers grabbed the menu. "I haven't eaten in at least an hour. I'm starving."

"Are you ever not hungry?" Colt joked.

Suddenly, Colt's phone lit up and buzzed on the table. It was a text from Andrea.

Meet me in the library ASAP!

Colt snatched up the phone before Bulldog could read the message. "I've got to bounce."

Bulldog's eyes widened. "We just got here, bro. If you leave who am I going to talk to?"

"You'll be too busy cramming wings into your mouth to talk. You won't even miss me."

Colt didn't want to let on where he was going. Ditching his teammate and heading to the library on a Friday night sounded pretty lame. But Andrea's text looked urgent. Colt's mind raced trying to make up a good excuse for leaving. He panicked.

"Something's come up at home. My mom needs help . . . cooking in the kitchen."

"Cooking?" Bulldog arched his eyebrows. "You can barely boil water, bro. Since when did you become a chef?"

"Oh, it's a brand new hobby for me," Colt said, putting on his jacket to leave. "You'd never guess how new."

The Edmonton library was six blocks from the

restaurant on the other side of downtown. Andrea's message sounded like an emergency. Colt didn't want to make her wait. He sprinted every block, streaking by the office buildings that towered overhead. He raced through the front doors of the library gasping for breath. His eyes darted left and right as he hurried through the stacks of books. No Andrea. His heart pounded as he reached into his pocket for his phone. He typed a short message:

Where r u?

The reply came instantly.

In the basement

The basement? Maybe she had fallen and hurt herself? Maybe some crazed janitor was holding her hostage in a broom closet, just like in one of those horror movies. He leaped down the stairs two at a time.

At the bottom Colt came face to face with a sign on the wall: ARCHIVES. He took a deep breath and stepped into the dark room. He was hit with an overpowering, musty smell. *This must be where they keep all the old newspapers and books*, he thought. He waited a few seconds for his eyes to adjust to the dim light. Then he saw a row of computer monitors, and a girl with long black hair sitting in front of a glowing screen.

"Andrea!" he whisper-called.

She waved him over without taking her eyes off the screen.

"So, why the emergency text?" he puffed.

"I was doing some research on my story about football injuries."

Colt nodded, his chest still heaving.

"And I found something you'll want to see."

Colt let out a long sigh. He was relieved to see his girlfriend was safe. But she was just looking at some old newspapers. *How big a deal could that be?* He doubted it was big enough to drag him away from Bulldog on wings night.

"Staring at some old papers in the dark doesn't sound very exciting," Colt said, rolling his eyes.

"You'd be surprised. And it's not just any newspaper." Andrea's dark eyes flashed. "It's the *Pittsburgh Post* from 1989."

Colt stared back at her. "That's about the time my dad played pro ball for the Pittsburgh Steelers."

"It was his last year on the team," Andrea said, nodding. "I've read all the stories about him. He had quite a reputation." With one click she zoomed in on the paper. "Check this headline."

Colt pulled his chair closer to the screen. TAYLOR ACCUSED OF HEADHUNTING. He raised his eyebrows. "My dad never talked about this. All I know was that he played linebacker with the Steelers for five years."

Andrea nodded again. "The story says he'd go after quarterbacks with his helmet. Hit them at the knees and sometimes even head to head. He was one mean dude back then."

"He still is," Colt muttered. He clammed up before saying anything else. He didn't want to make Andrea suspicious about how the Hurricanes' quarterback got hurt. He had to keep it secret.

"I hope you never play like that," Andrea said.

"Like what?"

"Like your dad did. Trying to hurt guys on purpose. I don't think I could ever have a boyfriend who did that." "I hope I never have to either," Colt said. But inside he worried that Coach might tell him to make another dirty hit.

Andrea focused back on the screen. "Did your dad ever tell you why he stopped playing football?"

"He never talked about it. I just figured he got too old."

"Then this is going to interest you," she said, clicking to another headline.

Colt read the words out loud. "CONCUSSION FORCES TAYLOR TO RETIRE."

"The story says he tackled the Denver Broncos' quarterback with a crushing helmet-to-helmet blow," Andrea said. "The pop from the two helmets hitting was so loud you could hear it all the way in the stands. They both got a concussion. But your dad got it worse. He was knocked out for a few minutes. They had to carry him off the field on a stretcher. After that he kept getting headaches that wouldn't go away. He never went back. That was the last game he ever played."

Colt's eyes grew wide. His jaw dropped. After all these years he was just finding out the truth about why his dad had to give up pro football. Why he became a high school coach. And maybe why he was still getting headaches.

6 MUTINY

"We're fifteen minutes late," Bulldog said, looking panicked.

"I know, I know, it's my fault," Colt replied, piling books into his locker. "I had to stay after English class for a lecture from Mrs. Drago. The Dragon Lady said if my grades didn't get better she'd have to tell my parents. And that's something I don't need. Coach is already one step away from making me stay on the bench for games. If he hears my marks are sucking, he'll make me stay at my desk for weekends, too." Colt snapped his lock back on and spun the dial.

Bulldog shook his head. "I wouldn't want to be you, bro. Let's head to practice."

Colt and Bulldog raced down to the locker room. They walked in like they always did. But something was wrong. The room was completely empty. There were no players. There was no coach. No one was putting on pads. No one was joking around. No one was playing music. It was quiet as a cemetery. They turned around and walked right out again.

Colt wondered what was going on. He glanced at Bulldog who looked just as bewildered. *Was practice cancelled?*

There wasn't much Colt could do about it. If there were no players it was going to be pretty hard to practice. Unless he wanted to run around the field just to stay in shape.

"You want to get suited up and run laps?"

Bulldog rolled his eyes. "You think I'm going to make this sumo-sized body run around that football field just for the fun of it? Get serious, bro."

"I'm with you, man," Colt said. "The best way to stay in shape is by playing. I only run laps when Coach tells me to. And Coach isn't here right now."

"Well, there's no sense staying if there's not going to be a practice," Bulldog said.

Colt nodded. "Let's cruise back to our lockers, get our homework, and head out. I should get started on my next book report, anyway."

The two teammates walked down the hall peering into empty classrooms. They passed wide open doors to the math room, music room, and chemistry lab. Then they approached the social studies classroom. The door was closed tight, but Colt could hear voices coming from inside.

He crept up to the door and spied through the window. There must have been thirty guys inside! Gunner,

Keegan, Sanjay, Jamal, and the rest of the team were all sitting at desks like it was a normal class. He waved Bulldog over to sneak a look. Bulldog's brown eyes bugged out of his head.

Colt burst through the door. "What's going on?"

Gunner stood up and smiled like he had been expecting them. "I see you tracked us down."

"Yeah, and I don't like what I found," Colt said. "Looks like you're having a secret team meeting without the captain."

"It's not so secret," Gunner said.

"What do you mean?"

"Coach told us in the locker room to meet here instead of practice."

"Without Bulldog and me?"

"Yeah, we all thought it was the best way."

"The best way to do what?" Colt demanded, crossing his arms.

"To pick another captain."

"What are you talking about?" Colt said. "All the players voted for me in training camp."

"Well, maybe it's time for another vote," Gunner shot back.

"Why?"

"Because that was before we knew."

Colt's blood started to boil. "Knew *what*?"

"That you won't follow Coach's orders. That you won't do whatever it takes to win."

Colt's eyes darted around the room. He wondered if everyone felt the same way. He spotted Sanjay sitting at the back.

"What about you, Sanjay? Are you part of this mutiny, too?"

"I think Gunner has some good points. A captain has to lead by example, dude. I don't think a captain who disobeys his coach is a very good example."

"So, that's it? You're just going to name someone else captain?"

"Not exactly," Gunner said. "Coach said we should choose a player to be a co-captain with you. We're just about to vote."

"Oh, and let me guess how many candidates there are?" Colt growled.

"Just one." Gunner smiled thinly.

"Yeah, I thought so." Colt narrowed his eyes. He wasn't surprised that Gunner was turning on him. He had already seen him play dirty. But he couldn't believe that Keegan, Jamal, and Sanjay would stab him in the back, too.

Gunner stood at the front of the class. "All those in favour of making me the co-captain raise your hand."

Every arm in the room shot up except for two. Colt and Bulldog kept their hands by their sides. They just glared.

"So, where is Coach, anyway?" Colt asked. "If he's behind all this, why isn't he here?"

"He went home with another headache," Gunner said. "You would have known that if you had shown up to practice on time. Something that a good co-captain like me did."

Colt led Bulldog out the door. He was burning up inside. He was still a co-captain, but he had lost the trust of his team. Now when he gave orders in the huddle he just didn't know who would follow them.

"I'll see you tomorrow, Bulldog."

"You taking the bus home?"

"Not today."

"It's a long way to your house, bro."

"I need the walk."

Colt swung his backpack over his shoulder. He worried about Coach getting another headache. It must have been a bad one for him to cancel practice. He wondered if they'd keep getting worse. Were all the hits he took as a player adding up to a constant string of headaches now?

He wasn't the same Coach he used to be. Colt was hurt that he would call for a vote on a co-captain. Lots of teams had co-captains, but still, Colt knew Coach must have thought he couldn't get the job done. That he wasn't good enough. It was hard to follow a coach who didn't believe in you. It hurt, too, that he was siding with Gunner.

His dad wasn't the same dad he used to be, either. They never went to football games together anymore.

His dad always said he was too busy. But Colt knew he wasn't. He just sat around the house on the weekends watching football on TV. He never asked Colt if he wanted to watch with him, though.

The team was different, too. Gunner had always just looked out for himself. But the rest of the guys all used to be a solid unit, on and off the field. Keegan and Sanjay and Jamal were his friends. Now they had just sat in a room and voted against him. Only Bulldog had stuck with him.

He felt let down — by Coach, by his team, and by his dad. This wasn't how his dad had taught him to act when he was younger. No matter how bad things got, his dad always told Colt to stand up for himself. To walk tall.

Colt trudged on, his shoulders slouching as he neared home.

7 HUDDLE MUDDLE

It was the last game of the regular season and the Fairmont Falcons were proving to be a tough flock of birds. Their offence flew down the field every time they touched the ball. But the Warriors had responded to everything they'd thrown at them.

Colt and Bulldog watched on the sideline as Keegan led the offence on another march into Falcon territory. Three steps away Gunner stood with Sanjay, Jamal, and the other defensive players.

"Pass it!" Colt shouted at Keegan. "Their defence won't expect it."

"What do you know about their defence?" Gunner called. "You barely know our defence."

Colt shot Gunner a look. He didn't like that Gunner questioned his game-smarts. And he didn't like that he was hanging out with the other defensive players.

On the next play Keegan threw a pass just like Colt had suggested, but the Falcon defender knocked the ball down.

"Incomplete!" the ref called.

"Just like I told you!" Gunner yelled. "We should have run the ball."

Colt kept his mouth shut as he watched the next play. Keegan handed off the ball and the running back blazed into the end zone for a touchdown. It was just as if Gunner had called the play. The Warriors now clung to a slim 21–20 lead. It was late in the fourth quarter. Colt snapped on his chinstrap ready to go in.

The Falcons returned the kick-off to their own thirty. Their passing attack started to peck away the yards. A ten-yard slant here, a fifteen-yard hook pattern there. Sanjay and Jamal ran all over the field trying to stop the green birds. But it wasn't working. Their receivers kept hauling in pass after pass.

The Falcons swooped down the field and now had a first down in the red zone. It was do-or-die for the Warriors. There was under a minute to play. The winner would go to the playoffs.

Colt raised his arm for a huddle. Bulldog, Sanjay, Jamal, and the rest of the defensive squad trudged over. They stood waiting for him to call the play.

"Here's what we're going to do," Colt said. "I think they're going to run the ball. So, I want everyone to play up close to the line to stop them."

All the players except one nodded at Colt.

"You're dead wrong," Gunner said. "You've been wrong all game. I think they're going to pass the ball."

Now the players nodded at Gunner.

"So which is it?" Sanjay asked, throwing up his hands.

"Yeah, we can't do both," Bulldog said.

Colt glared at Gunner. "Since when are you calling the defensive plays?"

"Since I became co-captain," Gunner said, glaring right back. "Maybe you remember the vote we took a couple days ago."

Colt took one big step and stuck his helmet right up in Gunner's grille. "Well, I say they're going to run."

Gunner didn't back down. "And I say they're going to pass." His facemask bashed against Colt's.

Colt pushed him away. Gunner struck back. He shoved Colt in the chest. But Colt wasn't going to let anyone push him around. He shoved Gunner right back. Now it was an all-out brawl. Hands turned into fists. Shoves turned into punches. Both players were swinging wildly trying to hit any body part — heads, arms, guts. It was a heavyweight bout. But instead of battling in a ring, they were fighting in the middle of the huddle!

The referee ran over blowing his whistle. "Break it up!" He stepped between the two fighters and pushed them apart. "What do you think you guys are doing? You're on the same team!"

Coach shouted from the sideline, "Timeout!"

"You've got thirty seconds to figure this out with

your coach," the ref said. "And I'm giving you a delay-of-game penalty, too. That means the Falcons will have the ball on your ten-yard line."

Colt could see Coach waving them over to the sideline. His arms were spinning so fast he looked like a propeller plane ready for take-off.

"I've never seen anything like it!" Coach shouted. "Two players fighting in their own huddle? That's crazy! Look at your hands."

Colt held up his fists. His knuckles dripped with blood from pounding against Gunner's helmet. Gunner's swollen hands were no better. The white tape on his fingers looked like it was stained with bright red ketchup.

"I should kick both of you guys out," Coach raged. "But this game is too important. Nothing's going to stop us from winning. Not even you two clowns."

Colt and Gunner hung their heads. "Yes, Coach."

"The Falcons only have time for one more play," Coach said. "I want you to be ready for a pass."

Colt shook his head. "But I think they're going to run."

"I don't care what you think, Colt. You made bad calls before and you're wrong now. I'm agreeing with Gunner."

The sides of Gunner's lips turned up into a big smirk.

"Looks like Coach and I are on the same page," Gunner gloated.

"I want Gunner to blitz when the ball is snapped and put pressure on their quarterback," Coach said. "Force him to make a mistake. Let's go!"

On the next play Colt watched the Falcons' quarterback grab the pigskin from the centre and drop back into the pocket. His eyes darted left and right, searching for an open receiver in the end zone. Colt hated to admit it, but Coach and Gunner were right. It was going to be a pass.

Gunner blitzed across the line of scrimmage and chased after the quarterback. Colt saw him charging with his arms over his head to block the throw. The quarterback was rattled. He had to get rid of the ball quickly before he was drilled. He tried passing high over Gunner's outstretched arms. The pigskin sailed through the air into the end zone. But instead of falling into the hands of the Falcon receiver, it was picked off by Jamal. The Warrior safety squeezed the leather and bolted all the way to midfield before a Falcon could tackle him.

The whistle blew. The final play of the game was over. Jamal was mobbed on the sideline by his teammates. The Warriors had held on to win, but it was no thanks to Colt. If they had followed his order the Falcons might have scored and won. Maybe he wasn't the best player to call the defensive plays. Maybe he shouldn't be co-captain. He didn't know what to think. All he knew was that getting orders from both Coach and Gunner would be hard to take as they headed to the playoffs.

8 GUNNED DOWN

"We dodged a bullet."

Coach stood in the middle of the field at the next practice. He was surrounded by the entire Warriors team. "We almost lost that last game. We have to play better. The playoffs start next week and we're going to have a big fight on our hands."

"Like the fight we had in our huddle?" Keegan kidded.

Coach's head whipped around. "Who said that?"

Keegan slowly raised his hand. "I did, Coach."

"You think that's funny?" he asked, pointing a finger. "You think because you're the quarterback you can crack jokes? Let me tell you something, Mr. Quarterback. Nobody jokes about the team. No one player is bigger than the team. Not even you."

Keegan looked down and nodded. "Got it, Coach."

"Any other smart-alecky comments?" Coach asked, hands on hips.

Only Bulldog had the courage to speak up. "I'm not

trying to be smart, Coach, but we're still not sure who's making the calls on defence."

Coach's face flushed red. "Gunner! Colt! Front and centre, now!"

Gunner stepped out from the pack. Colt followed, but stayed a few feet away. He still didn't trust Gunner after the brawl in the huddle.

"You guys are the leaders of the team," Coach said. "That doesn't mean you have to be best buddies. I couldn't care less if you talk to one another off the field. But it does mean you have to work together when you're on the field. Am I making myself clear?"

Gunner and Colt hung their heads and nodded.

"So, here's what we're going to do. Since each one of you is a co-captain, you'll split the duties."

"How are we going to do that, Coach?" Colt asked. "We both play defence. We're on at the same time."

"Gunner, you'll call the defensive plays in the first half of the next game. Colt, you'll call them in the second. And I don't want any fighting over it. Got it?"

Gunner and Colt spoke together. "Got it, Coach."

Colt breathed a sigh of relief. At least he was still a co-captain.

Coach blew his whistle. "Listen up. We had a lot of missed tackles against the Falcons. They were running right over us. That can't happen. But I've got a solution."

"I wonder what trick Coach has up his sleeve this time?" Bulldog said under his breath.

"It's an old pro drill we used when I played for the Steelers," Coach said. "It's called *running the gauntlet*."

Colt shot a glance at Gunner. He expected him to be stoked for a hitting drill. He knew he'd want to prove that it wasn't him missing tackles in the game. But Gunner wasn't even listening to Coach. He was craning his neck to follow a man walking along the sideline.

"I want everyone to form two long lines about six feet apart," Coach said spreading his arms wide. The players lined up across from each other creating a narrow path about twenty yards long. "That's the gauntlet. Now, I want a running back at the far end and a linebacker at this end."

"And then you want us to run at each other?" Bulldog asked.

"That's what I want," Coach said nodding. "Colt, start us off. See if you're worthy of being a co-captain. Tackle that running back!"

Colt strapped on his helmet and dug in at one end of the gauntlet. The speedy halfback held a ball in his arm and waited at the other.

"Go!" Coach shouted.

The halfback bolted from his end and rocketed between the two lines of players. Colt ran forward from his end. He knew he had him. There was no escape for the running back. He couldn't cut left or right. There was a human wall of players keeping him inside the gauntlet. Colt and the halfback had to keep running straight at each other. Halfway down the path Colt crouched low and crunched the halfback at the waist. The running back doubled over like a jackknife. He went down hard with a thud.

"Where was that in the game?" Coach barked. "I want to see more of that."

"Let me in there," Gunner said.

The next running back took off from the far end of the gauntlet. Gunner charged from the near side. He held his arms out front, ready to make the tackle. Gunner was bigger and stronger than the halfback. Colt knew he'd have no trouble bringing him down. Suddenly, Gunner's cleat got caught in the turf. He stumbled headfirst onto the grass. The running back hurdled over the face down linebacker and dashed to the end of the gauntlet where he spiked the ball to celebrate.

"Take that, Gunner!" he shouted.

Gunner lay flat on the field. He pounded his fist on the ground in frustration.

A man's voice called out, "You call yourself a football player?"

At first, Colt thought it was Coach. But he was just standing there shaking his head. It was another man. The one who had been watching Gunner from the sideline. He had crept up close to the gauntlet and was yelling at Colt's fallen teammate. He wore a green army jacket and was about the same age as Coach. His height, brushcut, and steely blue eyes all reminded Colt of Gunner.

"Is that the best you've got?" he yelled.

Gunner sat on the grass and stared up at the man. "No, sir."

"I didn't go on all those missions just to watch you stink up your practice. That's no way to honour a soldier who was fighting for you halfway around the world. You're just embarrassing yourself. And me."

The man marched off the field, leaving two rows of dropped jaws. The players broke ranks from the gauntlet and huddled around Gunner.

"That was harsh, man," Jamal said.

Bulldog nodded along with all their teammates. "Yeah, bro, you didn't deserve that."

Colt reached down and helped Gunner to his feet. "What was that all about?"

"I guess my dad is back from the army."

9 NUMBER FORTY-FOUR

Colt knew the real season was just beginning.

He thought back to the earlier games of September and October. The Warriors had won every clash. The victories never came easily, though. The players always had to have one eye on the game and one eye on Coach.

Keegan got the worst of it right from the start. After every incomplete pass Coach would yell at him. After every bad hand-off he'd let him have it during a time-out. But getting an earful must have worked. Keegan was now one of the best quarterbacks in the league. Playing defence was no picnic, either. Colt and Gunner were a two-man wrecking crew. The only problem was sometimes they swung at each other. Coach settled that once and for all. Now the two co-captains didn't waste energy talking to one another. They saved it for hunting down running backs and sacking quarterbacks.

The cold weather of November had arrived, but the competition was heating up. It was playoff time.

"Make no mistake, the Pembina Panthers are a

good team," Coach said. He stood with a clipboard in the middle of the locker room and addressed his troops. "They wouldn't be playing against us in today's semi-final game if they weren't."

Coach seemed relaxed. But after his outbursts in the last few weeks the team knew this was the calm before the storm. If the Warriors fell behind in the game the players didn't know what to expect. They had seen both sides of Dr. Jekyll and Mr. Hyde.

The players were still putting on their uniforms, but everyone stopped to listen. They knew Coach demanded complete attention.

"The Panthers play like a bunch of wild cats," he said. "Who thinks we can tame them?"

"We can, Coach!" Gunner called from the back.

"Who can?" Coach asked.

The entire team shouted as one. "WE CAN!"

"Is defeat an option?"

The players shot right back. "NO WAY, COACH!"

"That's right. We're winning this game no matter what. We're going to take it to them right from the opening kick-off."

"What's the game plan, Coach?" Keegan asked.

"There are four ways we're going to beat the Panthers, so listen up. Bulldog, that means you."

"I'm all ears," Bulldog said.

"And butt!" Sanjay yelled.

The room exploded with laughter.

Bulldog stood up from the bench and wiggled his backside.

"That's the worst dance I've ever seen," Jamal said, grinning.

"No," Bulldog said, now wiggling in a circle, "this is the worst dance you've ever seen."

When the laughter died down, Coach held up one finger. He hadn't even cracked a smile. "First, our offence has to be razor sharp. Every pass by our quarterback needs to be on the money."

"My arm feels strong," Keegan said, faking a throw.

Coach held up a second finger. "Our receivers have to haul in every ball."

"My fingers are like glue," Anthony Lee, the flanker, called out.

Coach held up a third finger. "Our defence has to be rock solid."

"We'll break up every pass," Sanjay said fist-bumping with Jamal.

Bulldog started in, "We might bend . . ."

". . . but we'll never break," Gunner finished.

Coach raised a fourth and final finger. "And last, we have to watch number forty-four. Tyrone Hill is the Panthers' star running back. He's big, he's tough, and he can gallop faster than a racehorse at the Kentucky Derby. He's gained over a hundred yards rushing each game this season. He's the most powerful weapon the Panthers have. And they're going to launch him again this afternoon. We have to do whatever it takes to stop him. Am I making myself clear, linebackers?"

"Yes, Coach!" Gunner shouted.

"Yes, Coach!" Bulldog yelled.

Colt felt the entire team was waiting for him to answer. He knew he had to say something. He was still a co-captain. He wanted to win like everyone else. But just how far was he willing to go?

"Last time I checked we had three linebackers," Coach said, scanning the room for Colt.

"Yes, Coach," Colt said quietly.

"That didn't sound like a guy who would do any-thing to win," Coach said. "Let's try that one more time. Will you do whatever it takes to stop number forty-four?"

Colt gritted his teeth and spoke a little louder. "Yes, Coach."

"That's what I like to hear."

Colt stared at the tiles on the floor afraid to look up. He knew every set of eyes in the room would be on him.

The players continued to suit up. Everyone had pre-game jitters. Gunner was the first dressed as usual and sat tapping his fingers on the bench. Keegan was rehearsing the plays he would call just like he was learning his acting lines. Bulldog started to get his game face on and snarled if anyone came near him. Sanjay and Jamal had earphones on listening to their favourite tunes. And Colt just tried to stay out of Coach's way.

There wasn't much talking. But that didn't mean the air was quiet. Familiar sounds shot through the locker room. Tape was ripped from large white rolls to wrap around injured wrists. Hard plastic shoulder pads were smacked by teammates to prepare for their first hit of the game. Cleats clicked on the hard, tile floor. When the last helmet chinstrap was clipped on and the final lace tied up, the Warriors were ready for battle.

Colt, Bulldog, and Gunner walked from the fluorescent glare of the locker room into the bright sunshine of the Woodside field.

It was showtime.

10 'SORRY DOESN'T CUT IT'

Two yellow school buses pulled into the Woodside parking lot. One was packed with cheering Panther fans. One was filled with Panther players in uniform.

Colt watched the black cats pour from the bus and run across the field. He didn't take it as a sign of bad luck, though. It was all good. He was pumped for the chance to play the Panthers.

The big cats formed a giant huddle at the fifty-yard line with their coach in the middle giving one last pep talk. Players leaped high. Fists punched the air. Cheerleaders flashed their pom-poms. The Panthers were on the prowl, hungry for playoff prey.

The Warriors marched onto the field two-at-a-time like a column of Roman soldiers. Colt felt like a gladiator entering the coliseum from centuries ago. Instead of facing a wild lion he was about to fight a team of ferocious Panthers.

He glanced at the bleachers and saw his mom waving. She didn't attend every game, but this was a big one. Andrea stood farther down the sideline. She paused from scribbling in her notebook and flashed a quick smile at Colt. He smiled back, more nervous about playing well in front of his girlfriend than his mom.

As co-captains, Colt and Gunner stood at centre field for the coin toss to decide the opening kick-off. The Panthers would get to make the call since they were the visiting team.

The referee flipped the quarter high into the air.

"Heads!" the Panther captain shouted.

The coin glinted in the sun before landing on the grass. "Heads it is," the referee said, leaning over to check it. "Your choice, Panthers."

The Panther captain pumped his fist. "We'll take the ball."

Colt smiled. He didn't mind his team kicking the ball to the Panthers to start the game. In fact, it was just what he wanted. The Warriors' defence was the best in the league. No team could run against three linebackers as strong as Bulldog, Gunner, and him. Even a team with a great running back like number forty-four.

The Warriors' defence lined up twelve strong across the field, ready for the kick-off.

Boom!

The ball sailed high through the clear blue sky, falling into the hands of the Panther return man deep in his own end. Colt and his teammates charged down the field, breaking through every block the Panthers tried to throw at them. The ball carrier was swarmed by Warriors. Black and blue uniforms surrounded him. He had nowhere to go. Bulldog let out a snarl as he tackled him at the twenty yard-line. It was only a ten-yard runback.

Colt high-fived his linebacker teammate. *This was going to be easy*, he thought.

It was the opening play of the game and Gunner raised his arm for a huddle. Colt joined his teammates in the circle. His hands rested impatiently on his hips waiting for Gunner to call the play. A play he'd rather be calling.

"Let's show them who's boss," Gunner said. "Watch for a run up the middle."

The Warriors lined up across from the Panthers. Both teams dug in. Gunner, Bulldog, and Colt spread out behind their four defensive linemen. Sanjay and Jamal paced in the secondary, waiting to cover their receivers. The Panther quarterback leaned over his centre and called the signals. He looked left. He looked right. Colt's eyes zeroed-in. He watched every twitch, trying to read the play. The quarterback grabbed the snap and handed the pigskin to his waiting halfback. It was the simplest call in the playbook. Colt clenched his fists. *This hand-off was going nowhere.*

The halfback tucked the ball in the crook of his arm and ran up the middle just like the play called for.

Colt scrambled to his right to plug the hole and wait for him. Bulldog and Gunner closed in from each side. They were going to stop this run cold. The Warriors would be sending the Panthers a message right from the start. *Don't mess with us.*

Colt was so confident he'd tackle the Panther ball carrier he forgot to do one thing. Check his number. He shot a glance at the halfback's jersey. Two yellow fours were charging right at him. It was Tyrone Hill.

Colt spread his arms wide to grab the shifty runner. *He could still bring him down.* But Tyrone saw the hit coming. He spun around and danced away from Colt's grasp, leaving him crashing to the ground. Colt looked up from the turf hoping Bulldog and Gunner would have better luck.

The two Warrior linebackers closed in from either side. Just as they were about to deliver their crushing blows the Panther halfback shifted into another gear and scooted between them. Instead of crunching Tyrone at the same time, Bulldog and Gunner hit only one thing — each other. Their bodies collided and collapsed to the ground.

Tyrone kept flying down the field. Sanjay and Jamal did their best to catch him, but the Panther speedster was long gone. He galloped the whole length of the field for a touchdown. Then he spun the ball like a top in the end zone to celebrate. Tyrone was mobbed by his Panther teammates.

The referee blew his whistle. After the convert the scoreboard read 7–0. The game was less than a minute old. The Warriors were already a touchdown behind.

Colt stood on the sideline with Bulldog and Gunner. He was in a state of shock. He had taken the Panther running attack too lightly. Colt vowed to make up for his mistake.

"Sorry, Coach," he said.

"Sorry doesn't cut it," Coach shot back.

"I'll bring him down next time."

"You better, or else."

Colt heard Coach's threat. He didn't know what he meant by it. And he didn't want to find out. He knew Coach would stop at nothing to win this game. It was all Coach had talked about all week. At breakfast he'd go on about the Panthers' strengths and weaknesses. He'd describe their favourite plays, and how to stop them. Then a weird thing would happen. That night he'd repeat the same thing at dinner. It was like he'd totally forgotten what he'd said.

The Warriors' offence sputtered and was forced to punt the ball back to the Panthers. Colt strapped on his helmet and jogged onto the field. This time the Warriors' defence knew they were in a war and battled harder. Their beefy front four plugged the middle while Colt, Bulldog, and Gunner darted from side to side, dragging down the speedy Panther running back.

They were keeping Tyrone Hill boxed in, stopping

him from racking up the yards. But just when they thought they had halted the Panthers' running attack, their quarterback would drop back and pass to one of their wide receivers. Sanjay and Jamal were no match for their size and speed. The referees kept signalling first downs. And the Panthers kept steamrolling down the field. The team with the jet black jerseys struck for two more touchdowns before the end of the first half.

Colt looked up at the scoreboard as he trudged off the turf. He shook his head. The Panters led 21–7. Maybe seeing black cats was bad luck, after all.

11 GOING TOO FAR?

"Sit down!" Coach barked.

It was an order. Every player grabbed a spot on the long bench.

Coach tugged hard on his blue Warriors' cap as he paced in front of Colt and his teammates. The other team was called the Panthers, but it was Coach who was stalking like a giant cat. His face was strained as he spat out his words. "Does anyone remember what I said about winning this game?"

Gunner was the only one who dared to speak up. "Losing wasn't an option, Coach."

"That's right. Not an option. I won't have it. If we lose this game we're finished. It means our undefeated regular season was all for nothing." He glared at the wide-eyed faces. "Is that what you guys want?"

The Warriors were still breathing hard, but found the strength to reply with one voice.

"No, Coach!"

"I didn't think so. That's why I was surprised by

what I saw on the field during the first half." Coach stopped in front of his hefty linebacker. "Bulldog, what word would you use to describe the way the team played?"

"Crap," Bulldog replied.

The tired Warriors nodded up and down the bench.

"Yeah, crap. I couldn't have picked a better word myself." Coach narrowed his eyes at Colt. "And who was leading Team Crap out there? Who was Captain Crap?"

Colt was burning mad. He knew he didn't play well, but it wasn't as if Gunner had played any better. It was just like Coach to pick on him in front of the whole team.

Halftime was almost over. The referees were back on the field. The game was about to start. If Coach had any more orders, he had to give them now.

"Keegan! Offence! Get out there and make me feel happy, not crappy."

Coach gave one last angry stare down the bench and stomped away. Like an army general he stood at the edge of the battlefield glaring out at the enemy.

Colt watched the Warriors' offence receive the kick-off to start the second half. Despite the tongue-lashing from Coach, Keegan still wasn't able to move the ball. He called two running plays that went no-where. The Panthers' defensive line was like a brick wall the Warriors couldn't break through. They would have to punt. Coach grabbed his head with both hands in disgust. Colt knew if Coach had a headache things were only going to get worse. He expected Keegan to get an earful when he got to the sideline.

The powerful Panthers' offence was about to get the ball back. Colt strapped on his helmet, ready to go in and face number forty-four.

All eyes were on the game. Everyone on the bench and everyone in the stands were watching the Warriors kick the ball. Everyone but Coach. He had his eyes on Colt.

"Get over here," he growled.

Colt wondered why Coach had picked this exact moment to talk to him. A time when no one was looking at them — not a player, not a ref, not a fan.

Colt pulled up beside Coach. His eyes were glazed over. He stared blankly across the turf at the Panther offence. "I want him gone."

"Who?"

"You know who," Coach said. "Forty-four. Stopping him is the only way we're going to win this game."

"I'll do my best to tackle him."

Coach glared. "From what I saw in the first half your best wasn't good enough. I'm not leaving this to chance." He reached out his big hand and smacked Colt three times on his helmet. Then he pointed to Tyrone Hill who was running onto the field. "I want you to take his head off."

Colt froze. His mouth wouldn't work. He couldn't believe what Coach was telling him to do.

"If you don't follow my orders, if you're not willing to do what I say, you can go and sit down right now. You'll be benched for the rest of the game. And for as long as I'm Coach. Do you hear me?"

Colt's heart pounded. His brain raced. Spearing another player with your helmet was the most dangerous play in football. It was also against the rules. Colt would get a penalty from the ref for sure. And a bigger penalty from Coach if he didn't. If he didn't follow orders he'd be letting down his dad and his team.

The referee blew his whistle to start the next play.

Colt's head was still reeling with confusion. He hated being blamed for the Warriors' bad playing. He would do almost anything to stop the Panthers from scoring. *But this? Was turning into a headhunter going too far?*

There was no time left to figure it out. He was running on animal instinct now. Not thinking — just reacting. Colt sprinted onto the field. He held up his hand and called for a defensive huddle. It was the second half and he was in charge now. His orders shot out like machine gun fire.

"Bulldog, you watch the quarterback in case he runs. Gunner, you cover the receivers for short passes in the flats."

Bulldog stared at Colt. "Don't you think you're forgetting someone?"

"Yeah, man. What about forty-four?" Gunner asked. "He's the only guy we have to stop."

Colt narrowed his eyes at Bulldog and Gunner. He wanted to make up for his bad play. He wanted to prove to the team he could do more. He wanted to prove to Coach he could do more.

"I'll take care of it."

The Panther quarterback took the snap and back-pedalled like he was going to pass. He cocked his arm to throw. But it was a fake. Instead, he handed the ball off to the running back who was hiding behind him — number forty-four. Most of the Warriors' defence had been sucked in by the draw play. Bulldog chased after the quarterback. Gunner stuck with the receivers. Both got caught out of position. Only Colt had read that it was a running play.

Colt burst through the Panther offensive line. His legs pumped like pistons. His eyes locked on the star running back. The target was in his sights. Tyrone Hill tucked the pigskin in his gut and charged downfield like a wild bull. He stampeded straight at Colt.

It all happened in a flash. Colt lowered his head and launched himself forward like a missile. He braced his neck and shoulders for the jolting hit that was to come. His helmet smashed into Tyrone's helmet with a jarring pop. It was a head-on collision between two speeding cars.

Tyrone's neck snapped back. His eyes rolled up into

his head. His arms and legs fell slack. The body that had been hurtling forward just seconds before came to a dead stop. Tyrone Hill crumpled to the ground, motionless.

12 EJECTED AND DEJECTED

Colt was laid out flat on the turf. Stunned.

He got up slowly, steadying himself on one knee. He looked around, dazed from the crushing blow. The players from both teams had formed a ring around the injured pair. Somewhere he heard a whistle blow. The referee waved at the Panther bench for help.

"Someone call an ambulance!"

It was all a blur.

A voice called out next to him. "Put your arm around my shoulder, bro."

Colt leaned on Bulldog and trudged woozily off the field. The two players walked towards Coach. Colt expected a high-five, a smile, or at least a nod. He had done what he had been told. He had taken out forty-four.

"That was a mean tackle," Coach said, shaking his head. "I don't know why you hit him like that."

Colt's jaw dropped. *Coach knows exactly why I did it.*

An ambulance drove onto the grass with its lights

flashing red and blue. Colt sat on the bench and watched two paramedics rush onto the field. Tyrone Hill was carried off on a stretcher. His head was strapped down so it wouldn't move. "A safety precaution," one of the paramedics said, "just in case his neck is broken."

The Panthers clapped for their injured teammate as he was whisked off the field. The Warriors did the same. They all knew it could be one of them next time.

The paramedics weren't the only ones paying attention to the injured player. The reporter for the school newspaper was waiting for them on the sideline. Andrea ran beside the stretcher asking the medical team questions about Tyrone's condition.

"Was he knocked out?"

"He was unconscious for a minute, but he's awake now."

"Can he talk?"

"He doesn't know where he is."

"Is it a concussion?"

"Could be. The doctors will have to examine him. We're just trying to get him to the hospital as soon as we can."

The paramedics carefully placed Tyrone into the back of the ambulance. The white emergency vehicle roared away, siren blaring into the late afternoon air. Andrea stood watching the ambulance disappear. She shot a glance at Colt and shook her head. She wrote a few more notes in her book. Then she walked away.

The referee blew his whistle, signalling the game to start again. But first, he had to make a call on Colt's tackle. He tapped the forearm of his striped jersey to indicate a penalty and pointed towards the Warriors. "We've got a personal foul against the Warriors' number fifty-five," he said. "That's a fifteen-yard penalty for spearing."

A fifteen-yard penalty isn't so bad, Colt thought. He'd be back in action just as soon as he recovered from the hit. But the ref wasn't finished. "And number fifty-five is ejected from the game."

Colt slumped on the bench. He had been kicked out. His game was over.

The penalty moved the Panthers fifteen yards down the field, but that was as far as they got into Warrior territory. Without their star running back the Panthers had lost their number one weapon. They had no fangs to bite into the Warriors' defence. Bulldog and Gunner shut down their second-string halfback every time he carried the ball. Their passing attack was grounded. Sanjay and Jamal covered their receivers like a blanket on every play. The Panthers had to keep punting the ball back.

The Warriors could sense the momentum was shifting. Suddenly, the game was going their way. Keegan guided the offence to two more touchdowns. The Warriors had closed the gap and now only trailed 24–21. It was late in the fourth quarter. The Panthers were running out of gas. Just holding on. No one could see that more than Coach.

"We're only down by three points!" He paced in front of the bench waving his hands wildly. "We can win this game! There's no stopping us!"

Coach called Keegan to the sideline. "I don't want any excuses! We're going in for the score." He shouted out a series of plays for the Warriors' quarterback to call and shoved him back onto the field.

Colt sat silently on the bench. Gunner was next to him on one side. Bulldog was on the other.

"I didn't think you had it in you, man," Gunner said. "You crushed that guy. It was awesome."

"I did what I had to do," Colt said. "Tyrone Hill was killing us."

Bulldog narrowed his eyes at Colt. "Yeah, but that didn't mean you had to kill *him*." He stood up from the bench and walked away leaving Colt behind.

Colt wanted to tell Bulldog why he'd done it. How he wanted to do what his dad told him to. But also how his dad couldn't remember telling him to make the hit. He wanted to do what was right. But he didn't know what was right anymore. It was all too hard to explain. No one would understand. Not even Bulldog.

With less than a minute to play Keegan tossed a thirty-yard pass to the Warrior flanker. Anthony made a fingertip catch at the ten-yard line and dashed into the Panther end zone for a touchdown. The comeback was complete. The Warriors had won 28–24. They were going to the championship.

13 TRAPPED

Colt knew the drill.

Andrea would pace outside the locker room like a hungry pit bull waiting for a bone. She had questions about the game and she wanted answers — now. She had to meet the deadline for the *Woodside Weekly*.

Colt knew she'd be fuming. She had been working on her story about head injuries for weeks. How they were happening more and more in high school football. And now this. She was an eyewitness to a helmet hit that sent a star running back to the hospital. Worst of all, she had seen her boyfriend do it.

The rest of the team was celebrating the victory, but Colt wasn't in a partying mood. He was still feeling a little woozy from the hit. Plus, getting kicked out of the game meant he didn't see any more action. Bulldog and Gunner had to work extra hard to make up for him not playing.

Even though the Warriors won, most of the players were concerned about the injured Panther.

"You nailed that dude," Sanjay said. "I hope he's all right."

Jamal nodded. "I've never seen a hit like that. I thought his head was going to pop off."

Sanjay and Jamal bumped knuckles with Colt, but that didn't make him feel any better. He had never wanted to hurt another player. He hated that. He hated Coach for making him do it. And then acting like he had nothing to do with it.

He shot Coach an angry glare. He was all smiles, laughing it up with Gunner, who had become his favourite player. He would do anything Coach said. No questions asked.

All Coach wanted was the win so the team could go on to the championship. He didn't seem to care about injuring the other team. Or that Colt might have been hurt from the dirty tackle as well. He could have been carried off the field just like Tyrone Hill.

Colt took his time getting dressed. He even spent two whole minutes tying up his kicks. If he had been on the field the referee would have given him another penalty for delay of game. He secretly hoped that if he waited long enough Andrea would give up and leave so he wouldn't have to face her. He was wrong.

By the end, it was just Colt and Coach left in the locker room. They had been avoiding each other the whole time. Bulldog, Gunner, Sanjay, Jamal, and Keegan had all split a long time ago.

Coach came out of his office and motioned to Colt. "Let's go," he said, walking to the locker room door. "Mom will have dinner on the table."

He swung the door open and came face to face with Andrea. Just like the players in the game, she hadn't given up. She didn't waste any time in hitting Coach with her first question. The words came flying out sharp as knives. "Is that the only way the Warriors can win, Coach?"

"I don't know what you're talking about."

"I think you do," she shot back. "The Panther running back was taken out on purpose. You went headhunting."

"Headhunting? Listen you, pint-sized princess, you don't even know what that means."

"Don't I?" Andrea asked. Her eyes were narrowed in suspicion. Her nostrils flared. Now she was in full pit bull attack mode. "Maybe no one else knows about you getting suspended for headhunting back in 1989 with the Steelers. But I do!"

Colt watched the blood drain out of his father's face.

"How do you know about that? That was a long time ago."

"I'm a reporter. It's my job to know."

"That's the way we played in the pros," Coach growled. He clenched his jaw so he wouldn't yell. "It's a man's game. People get hurt all the time. You wouldn't understand."

"The only thing I have to understand is a fifteen-year-old boy is lying in a hospital with a head injury."

"We're all sorry forty-four got hurt. It was an accident just like the quarterback hurting his knee in the other game."

"It sure didn't look like an accident," Andrea said. "It looked like Colt went out there to get him. Like he used his helmet as a weapon."

"Sometimes teenagers don't know what they're doing," Coach said.

Andrea's eyes blazed with anger. "So you're saying Colt did it by himself. That he went out there to hurt the Panther on purpose? That you had *nothing* to do with it?"

Coach nodded. "That's what I'm saying. I don't remember telling him to hit anyone." He pushed past Andrea and kept walking.

Colt felt like the walls of the hallway were closing in. On one side, his dad wasn't admitting to anything. Coach was acting like he'd never even talked to Colt. On the other side, Andrea was ticked off. She had a right to be. Colt also knew he was next on her attack list. She wouldn't go easy on him. She had no mercy when it came to reporting the truth. Andrea narrowed her dark eyes further and fired her next round straight at him.

"Tell me you didn't spear the Panthers' player on purpose, Colt. Tell me you believe in playing fair like you always say you do. Tell me your coach, your father, ordered you to hit Tyrone Hill in the head. Tell me he's the headhunter, not you."

By the end of Andrea's speech her eyes had started to glisten.

Colt was trapped. He couldn't reveal the truth to Andrea. Coach was standing just down the hall. He could hear every word. If Colt ever wanted to play football again, or have his dad trust him again, he couldn't blame him for the tackle. He couldn't admit that it was all Coach's idea. That his own father had ordered him to take out the Panther. Andrea would hate him. His father would hate him. Neither one might ever talk to him again.

Colt was at a complete loss for words. So, he looked straight ahead and walked right past his girlfriend.

"Hey, we're not done here, Colt. Where do you think you're going?"

"Home."

It was his only way out. Even though he knew things would be no better at home.

14 ALONE

Colt sat on the edge of the chair. His leg bounced up and down like a jackhammer.

The Edmonton High School Football League had called an emergency meeting. They had to decide if Colt should be suspended for his hit on the Panther running back. The trial was to be held in their office in five minutes.

He had taken a bus downtown after his last class at school. He didn't want to ride in the car with Coach. There had been nothing but dead air between them during the drive home after the game.

They had stayed out of each other's way at home, too. Colt ate dinner watching TV while Coach sat with his mom at the kitchen table. Then, when Coach came into the living room to watch a detective show, Colt disappeared into his bedroom. He wanted to finish some homework and then chill playing a video game. When Coach zigged, he zagged.

Colt was shown into a meeting room. A half-dozen

black chairs were spaced around a table. One by one the chairs were filled by the league president, the referee, and other league officials. After a few minutes there was only one empty chair. Coach still hadn't arrived.

Colt kept his head down and stared at the table. He was worried about the meeting. Should he say Coach ordered the hit? Or should he say he did it all himself? He knew it must look bad. But he didn't know how he could blame his dad, even though his dad had been blaming him.

Coach finally walked in. "Sorry I'm late. I got lost driving over. I thought I knew the address, but I guess I forgot."

Colt watched him give the president a big smile like he had nothing to hide.

The president shook his hand and sat down to start the meeting. "I want to thank you all for coming on such short notice. This is an important matter and it deserves immediate attention."

"I couldn't agree more," Coach said.

"First things first," the president said. "How is Tyrone Hill?"

A woman sitting beside Colt checked her notes. "The medical report from the doctor says he's got a concussion and will be kept in the hospital another day for observation."

"A concussion?" Coach asked. "That's serious."

"Very serious," the president said, narrowing his

eyes at Colt. "Spearing with your helmet is a dangerous play and we can't allow it in this league."

"I couldn't agree more," Coach said.

Colt's eyes grew wide with shock. Coach was acting like he didn't believe in spearing. Like he had never done it in the NFL. Like he had never told Colt to do it. But Colt felt powerless to say anything. Who was the league going to believe, after all? A head coach who used to play in the National Football League, or a fifteen-year-old kid?

"Let's review what happened," the president said.

"Here's the way I saw it," the referee said, looking across the table at Colt. "The middle linebacker for the Warriors went straight for the head of the Panther running back with his helmet."

"Did it look like an accident?" the president asked.

"Not a chance," the ref said, shaking his head. "The Warriors' player was on a mission. His only goal was to knock the head off of number forty-four. It was sickening."

The president folded his hands together on the table. "It seems clear the Warriors' Colt Taylor was responsible for hitting the Panther running back and giving him a concussion. All that's left to determine is if he was ordered to do it."

"I take that as an insult!" Coach roared, pounding the table. "Don't you think I'd remember ordering something as awful as a spear to the head? I want my team to win as much as the next coach. But not at any cost. I didn't even talk to Colt before the play."

"Please calm down, Coach Taylor," the president said, holding up his hands. "We just want to get to the bottom of this." He turned to Colt. "Is what Coach says true? Did you decide to hit the Panther running back all by yourself? Or did he tell you to do it?"

Colt's heart pounded in his chest. His hands started to sweat. He was confused. He didn't know what to think. What if his dad was telling the truth? What if he really didn't remember ordering the hit? He couldn't blame his dad for something he didn't even know he did. But the league could. What would happen if he told them what actually happened?

"It was me, sir. I did it myself."

"You're sure?" the president asked, giving Colt a chance to change his story.

Colt hung his head. "I'm sure."

The president gave a stern nod. "Then you leave us no choice but to suspend you for the championship game next week. This hearing is over."

The meeting room door opened. Colt walked through it in a daze. He looked straight ahead like a zombie. Not left, or right, or at his dad. He had to escape.

He could hear the league president talking to a reporter in the hallway. The reporter's voice sounded familiar.

Andrea had found out about the meeting. She had the president cornered and was drilling him with questions. "Will there be a suspension?" she demanded.

"Yes."

"Will it be for the coach or the player?"

"We've decided the coach was innocent, but the player was to blame. As a result of our findings, Colt Taylor will be suspended for the final game."

Andrea stopped writing in her notebook. Her pen dropped to the floor. She glanced at Colt with the saddest look he had ever seen.

Colt walked towards her. He needed to talk to someone who believed in him like Andrea always did.

"I had no choice," he said, reaching out to her.

"You always have a choice, Colt. And you made the wrong one. As far as I'm concerned you deserve the suspension."

"Let's get out of here and talk about it, Andy."

"I want to leave too. But not with you, Colt. I can't believe you did this. Not after everything we found out about your dad and concussions. From now on you're on your own. We're done."

Colt watched Andrea walk away and step into the elevator. She turned and looked right through him like he was a ghost. Then she vanished behind the closing doors.

15 THE BUZZ

News spread through the school like wildfire.

Did you hear? Did you hear? The best player on the Warriors has been suspended for the championship game! *Yeah! The coach's own son!*

The corridors buzzed with students and staff unable to believe what had happened. From the moment he entered school that morning Colt couldn't take one step without someone throwing an insult at him.

"We can't win now," a boy said, shaking his head as he walked by Colt's locker.

"I didn't know the Warriors were such dirty players," a cheerleader sneered in the cafeteria.

Even Principal Holly wagged a scolding finger as she passed him in the hall. "You've made our whole school look bad, Colt."

Every accusation stung. He kept his mouth shut, though. He tried to lie low by sitting by himself in the back of each class. But even the teachers wouldn't leave him alone.

In Biology, Mrs. Wyatt took the opportunity to explain how dangerous a blow to the head can be. "The kind of hard knock Colt gave the other player can result in a concussion," she said, holding up a large drawing of the brain. "That can mean a short-term loss of brain function, and that's not good." Colt winced upon hearing the words. He hoped Tyrone Hill's brain was working the way it should be.

In Physics, Mr. Swarbrick calculated the force of the two helmets colliding. "Colt's hit was almost a hundred times stronger than gravity!" he said, amazing even himself. When the bell rang Colt rushed to the front of the class and erased the numbers on the blackboard. He didn't want any reminders of the awful tackle.

In Language Arts, the Dragon Lady breathed a bit of fire his way. "I don't know what kind of young man does what you did, but he must be someone of questionable character. Someone you can't turn your back on. Someone you can't trust. If I were Coach I'd kick you off the team for good. That's what I'd do," she snorted.

Back at his locker Colt checked his phone for messages from Andrea. He didn't really expect to get one now that she had broken up with him. Most days she'd send him a text just to say hi, or to plan where they'd meet for lunch. But she wouldn't want to eat with him today, that's for sure.

By the time noon rolled around Colt didn't think

he had a friend left in the world. He grabbed his sandwich from his locker and headed to the cafeteria. With Andrea out of the picture he went to sit at the table where all the football players usually hung out. Jamal was already there sitting with Sanjay. They were laughing at a joke until Colt sat down. Then their faces soured like they were sucking on lemons.

"You're hurting the team," Jamal said. "We always trusted you to do the right thing. But getting suspended for the championship? What were you thinking, man?"

Sanjay agreed. "You could have hit him fair and square. We don't need that kind of dirty play on our team. Everybody thinks we're cheaters now."

Both players got up and moved to the end of the long table. They didn't want to be seen talking to the troublemaker.

Bulldog's beefy frame plumped down. His bulging lunch bag was twice the size of anyone else's. Before taking a bite out of his triple-decker ham and cheese sandwich, he turned to Colt. "When Coach said we should do anything to win, I don't think he meant spearing another player in the head. I know he told us to go after the knees of the Hurricane quarterback in that earlier game, but this was different."

"Don't be so sure," Colt shot back. "You don't know everything about Coach."

Bulldog raised his eyebrows. "What do you mean?"

Colt was desperate to tell his friend the truth, but

knew he couldn't. "Nothing. Forget I said anything." He clenched his jaw.

"We had a pact to play clean," Bulldog said, shaking his head in disgust. "Now you've gone and broken that. You let me down, bro."

"I know I did," Colt said. "One day I'll tell you why. But not today."

"I'm glad they suspended you," Bulldog said. "You don't deserve to play in the final game."

A voice shot through the cafeteria. "You did the right thing, dude."

Who could possibly think what I did was right? He looked around and saw Gunner coming towards him with a tray full of french fries. *Of course, it has to be Gunner.*

"Have a fry," Gunner said.

"I'm not hungry."

"I don't know what the big deal is," Gunner said. "So, you hit some guy on the other team with your helmet and now his head hurts. So what? At least we won the game. That's the important thing."

"Are you kidding me?" Bulldog said. "You can't go around hurting people on purpose. That's just wrong. You're no better than Colt." The big linebacker picked up his lunch bag and slid down the bench to join Jamal and Sanjay.

"Hey, where are you going?" Gunner asked. "Stay here with my buddy, Colt. We're just about to plan our next headhunting mission."

Colt could understand why Bulldog thought he was just like Gunner. How he would do anything to win — even injure a player. After all, that was what people saw him do out on the field. But he was sick of people thinking that and wished it would all go away. He needed the truth to be told. There was just one problem. He couldn't tell it.

16 PRESS PLAY

"I don't have time for this," Coach complained.

"Then you're going to have to make time," the league president said sternly.

The president had made a surprise visit to Colt's school. He sat in the small office of the *Woodside Weekly* newspaper. He had demanded three people attend the urgent meeting — Colt, Coach, and Andrea. Colt could understand why he and Coach had been asked, but wondered what Andrea had to do with it.

Everyone crowded around a table. A large computer sat in front of them. The screen was black, but ready to be viewed.

The atmosphere was tense. Coach wouldn't look at the president or Andrea. He knew neither one liked him. Colt wouldn't look at Coach or Andrea. He wanted to glance at Andrea more than anything, though. But he knew she must still be mad at him for getting suspended. He didn't blame her. All four looked around the room pretending the others weren't there.

Coach was fidgety and broke the ice. "The championship game is tomorrow. I've got to get my team ready. I don't have time to waste on dumb meetings like this."

"I can assure you this meeting is anything but dumb," the president said.

"Didn't we clear up this whole headhunting issue at your office last week?" Coach asked.

"We did. But things have changed," the president said.

"You suspended Colt for his hit on the Panther running back. What else could be different?"

"We've received new evidence."

"Like some cop show on TV?" Coach asked.

"Sort of," the president said. "And just like a detective show we want to find out who's guilty."

Coach leaned in. "So, what's the new evidence about?"

"We believe someone ordered the hit," the president said.

"No one told Colt to hit forty-four," Coach said. "He did it all by himself. Like I said last week, it was the reckless act of a stupid teenager."

"We disagree," the president said. "We now think someone told him to do it."

Coach raised his eyebrows. "Who?"

"You."

"Me? I never even talked to him before the hit."

"That's where you're wrong, Coach," Andrea spoke up. The small reporter had been quiet as a mouse. Now she roared like a lion.

"Who invited her, anyway?" Coach said, scowling at Andrea.

"I did," the president said. "Someone sent Miss Wong a very interesting video. And she did the right thing by bringing it to my attention."

"A video of what?" Coach demanded.

Andrea's expression turned furious. "Of you telling Colt to hit Tyrone Hill in the head. That's what!"

"I don't believe it," Coach said. He pushed his chair back from the table and crossed his thick arms.

"Then maybe you'll believe this," Andrea said.

She clicked the mouse and the computer flashed to life. The screen was all set to show a video. She pressed play. It looked like someone had used a smartphone to take a video from the bleachers next to the Warriors' bench. The picture was a little shaky, but there was a clear view of Coach. He was standing on the sideline during the game against the Panthers. It showed him hitting Colt three times on the helmet with his hand. Then he pointed across the field at the Panther running back. Coach's voice could even be heard saying, "Number forty-four." The last image was of Coach pushing Colt onto the field just before the spearing play. The whole video was no more than twenty seconds long, but it seemed to Colt like it played for ages.

From the corner of his eye Colt watched his dad view the video. At first, it was clear he was angry finding out that someone had secretly taken a video of him. But then something changed. Like a switch was flipped. When he saw himself hitting Colt on the head his jaw dropped. Lines of pain crept across his forehead. Then when he watched himself point at number forty-four his body recoiled back into the chair. He even shut his eyes for a split second. It was like he couldn't believe it was really him in the video.

The room was dead quiet after the video froze on the final shot.

The president pressed his lips together and glared at Coach. "I only have one question. And I only want one answer. Is that you telling Colt to hit the Panther player in the head? Yes or no?"

Coach spoke slowly. He seemed to be in shock from seeing himself in the video. "I can't believe that's me. I don't even remember talking to Colt. I would never hit my son like that."

"Well, I'm afraid it was you," the president said grimly. He looked Coach square in the eyes. "Yes or no."

Coach nodded sadly. "It must be."

The president turned his attention to Colt. "Is that true Colt? Did your coach order you to hit Tyrone Hill in the head?"

Colt sat silently. He took a long look at his coach.

The man who had told him what to do. The man who had been telling him what to do since he was a little boy. He didn't see a coach filled with anger. A coach who would do anything to win like ordering a vicious hit. All he saw was his dad. A dad who couldn't even remember what he had done.

"It's okay to answer," the president said. "You're safe here. I just want to know the truth."

Colt took a deep breath. "I didn't want to hit him, sir. It's not how I play." He locked eyes with Andrea. He wanted her to know that it wasn't his choice to head-hunt the Panther player. That she could believe in him again. "But I had to follow my dad's orders."

Coach slumped in his chair. He looked tired. His face was no longer clenched. His eyes no longer fiery. The trial was over. He had been found guilty.

Colt's dad started to stand up. "Are we done here?"

"Not yet." The president tightened his tie before making his final decision. "I have a few things to say. I know there's a lot of pressure to win. But winning should never come at the cost of injuring another player. Doctors are finding out that blows to the head can cause problems years after the hit."

Andrea nodded. "That's why I'm reporting on concussions in high school football. Players just like Tyrone Hill are ending up in hospitals all across the country. It's just lucky Colt didn't hurt his head in the game. Otherwise he might have a concussion, too."

"We need more stories like that," the president said. "Coaches, players, and fans need to know the dangers. Even Hall of Fame running back Tony Dorsett from the Dallas Cowboys has been diagnosed with a brain injury. He's in bad shape from all the head hits he got while playing."

Coach's brow furrowed with concern. He leaned forward. "TD has a brain injury? I was one of those guys who hit him in the head. Man, we had some battles. But to think I helped cause his brain injury makes me feel awful. He was one of the best." Then he glanced around the table at Andrea and the president. "I guess there's nothing left to say. It's all right there on the video. Give it to me straight."

"After reviewing the facts, I'm reversing my decision from last week," the president said. "Coach, you're officially suspended for ordering the hit. But Colt, you're cleared to play in the championship game."

17 I SPY

"Check this out," Andrea said, pointing at her laptop screen. "It's a story about that old NFL player, Tony Dorsett."

Colt slid closer on the couch and listened as Andrea read.

"It says Dorsett suffers from terrible headaches."

"Sometimes my dad has to go home from school they're so bad."

"And Dorsett has trouble remembering things, too."

Colt nodded. "Like when my dad forgot his way to the league meeting."

"Yeah, and sometimes it gets worse," Andrea said. "Sometimes Dorsett totally forgets where he is or what he's doing."

"Like ordering a terrible hit in a football game," Colt murmured.

Andrea squeezed Colt's hand and read on. "It says Dorsett gets frustrated a lot. And then he gets mad and loses his temper. But he can't help it."

"Sounds like my dad, all right. It's the way he's been acting all season, on the field and here at home."

Andrea read the end of the story. "Doctors say it can happen when you've had too many hits to the head. More and more retired football players are suffering from it all the time. They're working on new ways to treat it."

"I don't know why I didn't figure it out sooner," Colt said, shaking his head.

Andrea shot him a look. "Are you a doctor?"

"No."

"Are you a reporter always digging up the facts like me?"

"No."

"Well, it's no wonder you couldn't tell."

"Still, I should have known something was wrong. He's my dad."

"You can't blame yourself, Colt."

Colt's mom came into the living room from the kitchen where she had been cooking dinner.

"Is Dad home yet, Mom?"

"Not yet. I'm starting to get a bit worried. Especially after the day he's had. He phoned after your meeting and told me the news. He sounded upset with himself, which is unusual for your father. He always tries to be the big, tough football player. But today there was something different in his voice. He seemed quieter."

"I hope he's all right," Colt said. He wondered if his dad might be getting lost driving home.

"I think I'd better be going," Andrea said. "I'm sure Coach doesn't want to see me. He sure doesn't like me much."

"I don't think he's liked anyone this season," Colt said. "Me included. But we're starting to understand why."

Colt heard Coach come in from the garage.

"I'm home!"

"That's a relief," his mom sighed.

When Coach walked in Andrea scooted right by him. "See you tomorrow, Colt."

"There's no need to hurry home on my account, Andrea. In fact, you're welcome to stay for dinner."

Colt and Andrea both looked at Coach with surprise.

"I know I've been tough on you, Andrea," Coach said. "I should have been nicer. Your stories on head hits and concussions are just what the school needs. Keep up the good work."

Andrea grinned as she waved goodbye. "I will, Coach. And thanks. But I do need to get home. See you later, Colt."

Colt's mom brought over a steaming bowl of spaghetti and set it on the table. All three sat down and started to dig in.

Coach looked up from his plate. "Andrea's not the only one I haven't been nice to." He shifted his gaze between Colt and his mom. "I know I've been tough to live with. And tough to play for. Some days my head hurt so much I would go into a daze. I'd just get mad at anyone who got in my way . . . Colt . . . Bulldog . . . Keegan. I didn't know why. I thought it was just the stress of trying to win. But I found out today it's something more. When the league president said other NFL players had brain injuries from being hit in the head, I knew the same thing was happening to me."

"That must have been a scary feeling, Sam."

"It was, but not as scary as what I saw on the video."

His mom tilted her head and asked, "There was a video?"

"Yeah, someone in the stands took a video of me telling Colt to spear the Panther player. When I saw myself hitting Colt in the head I couldn't believe it. It was terrible, like a bad dream. I can't even remember doing it. I should probably thank the person who took the video. They made me realize how out of control I've become."

Colt's mom took her smartphone out of her purse and laid it on the table. "Then you can thank me."

Colt was so shocked he dropped his fork on the plate.

"Very funny," his dad said.

"It's no joke, Sam," his mom said, shaking her head. "I felt like a secret agent taking the video, but it was the only way I could show you how mean you'd become this season. You weren't the Sam Taylor I married years ago. All the headaches, the angry outbursts, the forgetting. I was worried about your health."

His dad gently reached across the table. "I'm ready to do what you've been suggesting all along."

His mom's small fingers disappeared into his large hand. "I'll make an appointment with the doctor."

"It can be any time since I'm not coaching now."

His mom frowned. "You must be disappointed to be missing the big championship tomorrow."

His dad nodded. "It's all I've thought about since the season started."

"I know it is, Sam."

"But I don't deserve to coach the game. Not after what I did to Colt."

Colt spoke up right away. "You didn't know what you were doing, Dad. You don't even remember talking to me."

"That's no excuse. To smack you on the helmet. To send you out there to hurt another player. That's terrible. I sure hope Tyrone is all right. And to risk my own son getting hurt? If you had been injured I never would have forgiven myself. It was the worst thing I've ever done. I still can't believe I did it. And for you to follow my orders . . . well I can't believe that either."

"But you're my dad," Colt said, locking eyes with his father. "You've been telling me the right thing to do since I was a little kid. I've been trying to be like you my whole life. I had to do what you said. I had to trust you."

Coach's eyes softened. Colt could see the pain on his face. He wasn't being his coach now. He was back to being his dad.

"I know you did."

18 STAND-UP GUY

Kick-off for the championship was only an hour away.

Colt had been jumpy all day. He couldn't wait for his last class to end. Finally, the Dragon Lady stopped talking. The bell rang. Now he could get ready for the big showdown with the Highland Hurricanes. He always found it harder waiting for the game than playing it.

He walked into the locker room not knowing what to expect. The last time he saw his teammates they wouldn't talk to him.

Bulldog's wide body stepped in front of him. His hands were clenched out front like they were ready to deliver a punch. Colt tensed and got ready to defend himself.

"Welcome back, bro." His oldest friend reached out a beefy fist for a knuckle-bump. "Andrea's story in the *Woodside Weekly* explained everything."

"But did you have to hit Tyrone?" Jamal asked, throwing up his hands. "Did you have to follow Coach's orders?"

Sanjay moved beside Jamal. "Yeah, couldn't you make your own decision?"

Bulldog stepped in. "I've got a question for you guys. What if someone told you to do something? Something bad. Would you do it?"

Jamal shook his head. "No way, man."

"Okay, but, what if that someone was your dad?" Bulldog asked.

Jamal nodded slowly after a moment. "You're right. My dad is the law. What he says, goes."

"I hadn't thought about it like that," Sanjay said. "I guess you had no choice."

Both players reached out and fist-bumped Colt. The team was back together.

"It must have been hard keeping it a secret," Jamal said.

"Brutal," Colt said. "It was awful thinking all you guys hated me. But I couldn't tell anyone. I didn't want to get benched. I wanted to keep playing to help the team. And I didn't know how to do that except by trusting my dad. I'm glad it's all over."

There was only one teammate who didn't bump fists with Colt.

"Now we don't have a chance," Gunner sneered.

"What are you talking about?" Bulldog said. "We're lucky to have Colt back in the lineup."

Gunner glared at Colt. "But we lost Coach. And we can blame your reporter girlfriend for that. She didn't have to send that video to the league. She wanted to get Coach kicked out of the game. She's a traitor."

Colt couldn't let Gunner get away with badmouthing his girlfriend. He didn't want to fight him right before the big game, but he felt he had no choice.

"You don't know what you're talking about," Colt growled. He gave Gunner a two-handed shove square in the numbers.

Gunner cocked his fist, ready to hammer Colt.

"That's enough!"

Every head in the locker room whipped around to face the door.

It was Coach.

"You're just in time to watch me drop your son," Gunner said, waving a fist in the air. "It was him and his traitor girlfriend that got you suspended. But don't worry, Coach, I've got your back."

"Sit down, Gunner," Coach said. He pointed to the end of the bench as far away from Colt as possible. Gunner griped, but did as he was told.

Bulldog looked puzzled. "I didn't think you were allowed to be here, Coach."

"I'm not allowed to coach during the game. But the rules don't say anything about me talking to you before the game here in the locker room."

"It's a good thing you are here, Coach," Gunner said. He looked boiling mad after taking on Colt. "Tell us again how we have to do whatever it takes to win.

Even if that means taking off some guy's head."

Coach rolled up the sleeves of his Warriors' wind-breaker. He rested one foot on the bench. Colt was looking at a different man. A man who wasn't about to coach a championship game. Who didn't have to win at all costs. This was a man in control. There would be no outbursts, no forgotten orders today.

Coach spoke calmly. "I want you all to listen to me. Especially you, Gunner."

Bulldog took a break from taping up his hands. Jamal stopped putting on his shoulder pads. Colt finished pulling on his jersey. Every player sat down and fixed his eyes on Coach.

"This is the biggest game of your lives, men."

"You know it!" Gunner shouted, jumping to his feet.

"But it doesn't mean we do anything to win."

Gunner sat back down. His brow wrinkled with confusion. "What are you saying? We should play to lose?"

"Not at all," Coach said. "We play hard. We give everything we've got on every play. We sacrifice for our teammates. We leave it all out on the field. But we play fair. We never use our helmets to go after a player's knees. And we never go after a player's head. Ever."

Gunner's jaw dropped. He looked dazed. His face was pale. His football world had been turned upside down.

Coach walked past Gunner to where Colt sat on the bench. "What I ordered Colt to do in the last game was wrong," he said to the players. "The league was right to suspend me. But I learned some things about myself. Some things I'm learning to live with. And I'll never ask any of you to make a dirty hit again. And if I do, I want you to refuse to do it until I'm myself again."

"There's still one big question, Coach," Bulldog said. "If you're not going to coach the game, who is?"

"I've decided to put one of you in charge," Coach said, scanning the faces in the room. "The toughest and fairest player on the squad. The Warrior with a heart like a lion."

Coach motioned for Colt to get up.

"The son who makes his father stand a little taller."

A shot of pride surged through Colt's body. His dad hadn't praised him for a long time. And never in front of the team.

Coach put his hand on Colt's shoulder. "This is your coach today. Colt will make the defensive calls when he's on the field. And help Keegan make the quarterbacking calls when he's waiting with the defence on the sideline."

"What about me?" Gunner demanded. "I'm a co-captain, too."

"Sorry, Gunner. When I said do whatever it takes to win, I was out of line. This isn't pro football, and it isn't twenty years ago. In this game you take your orders from Colt."

Colt heard some grumbling nearby.

"Coach made a bad call telling Colt what to do before," Jamal said. "So why should we trust him to make a good call now?"

Keegan nodded. "I'm glad Colt is playing. But should he be coach, too?"

Bulldog looked Keegan and Jamal in the eyes. "Who was the best player on the team before that hit? The player who made tackle after tackle? The player who got us to this game?"

"Colt," Keegan said.

"And who was the player that did what Coach asked? Who put his team before himself? Who took the blame and got suspended even though it wasn't his fault?"

"Colt," Jamal agreed.

"Exactly, bro. So who's the best guy, the most loyal guy, to lead us in this game?"

Keegan and Jamal both nodded and pointed at the new coach.

The clock on the wall ticked closer to the opening kick-off. Colt and his dad stood at the door patting each player on the back as they left for the field.

"You can do this," said the old coach.

"We can do this," said the new one.

19 BLINDSIDED

It was the rematch of the year. Colt knew the Hurricanes wouldn't have forgotten the last game between them. The Warriors had come back to win after the Hurricanes' star quarterback had been cut down at the knees. Colt was sure the pain of that play burned in Travis Valiant's memory. If anyone had motivation to beat the Warriors this afternoon, it was him.

"Heads!" Colt called. He and Gunner stood at midfield facing the two Hurricane co-captains.

"Tails!" the ref called, picking up the coin.

The Warriors had lost the toss. Colt hoped it wasn't a bad omen. The Hurricanes would receive the ball.

The stands were packed. Half the fans were cheering for the home-team Warriors. Half were rooting for the Hurricanes. Colt's mom and dad were watching somewhere in the crowd. Everyone roared as the Warriors booted the ball to start the game.

The Hurricanes were pumped. A wave of red uniforms came storming down the field right at Colt and his teammates. After a blazing forty-yard runback, Travis took over the Hurricanes' offence at mid-field. He masterminded a drive that even the three best linebackers in the league couldn't stop.

Colt, Bulldog, and Gunner never knew what play was coming next. When they expected a run, Travis would step back in the pocket and fire a perfect spiral to one of his wide receivers. When they expected a pass, he'd hand off the ball to his running back who'd scoot between them for a first down. After just four plays the Hurricanes had run the pigskin into the Warriors' end zone for a touchdown. Colt watched the convert sail through the goalposts. It was already 7–0.

In the second quarter the Warriors battled their way back. Slowly but surely the black and blue offence marched down the field into enemy territory. Keegan kept the Hurricanes guessing. Pass . . . run . . . run . . . pass. After two more short running plays they pounded the ball down to the one-yard line. But now it was third down. Even though they could smell the goal line it was risky to go for the touchdown. If the Warriors didn't score on their last down, the Hurricanes would take over the ball. Keegan called a timeout and ran to the sideline to talk over the next play with Coach Colt.

"Maybe we should kick a field goal and get the easy three points," Keegan said.

Colt looked him in the eye. "We need a touchdown to tie up the game. I think we should go for it.

I know you can do it." Colt pushed his quarterback back onto the field just like he had seen his dad do so many times before.

Keegan took the snap from the Warriors' centre and tossed the ball to his running back. He swept around the right side. His legs churned faster and faster. The Hurricane defenders dove at his feet, but all they tackled was turf. He raced across the goal line for the touchdown! The Warriors had taken the gamble and made it count. Colt punched the air on the sideline. The score was knotted 7–7.

Colt snapped on his chinstrap ready to go on for the kick-off. Suddenly, a voice shouted behind him.

"Let's go, Greg!"

Colt's head snapped around. A man in a green army coat was yelling at Gunner. His dad was back.

"What are you doing here?" Gunner asked.

"I couldn't miss this game, Greg. I know how much it means to you. I got special permission from the base to be here."

Gunner shot a glance over his shoulder as he and Colt headed onto the field.

"Remember, Greg, everything you've got!"

As the clock ticked down in the first half the Hurricanes' quarterback showed the crowd why he was an all-star.

Travis Valiant moved his red squad down the field with the precision of a surgeon. Every pass knifed deeper into the heart of Warrior territory. Every run cut further into their confidence. Colt and his teammates tried everything to stop the bleeding, but nothing worked. Travis was about to stab the Warriors with another touchdown.

Colt raised his hand for a huddle. "We have to stop him."

"But how?" Bulldog asked, shaking his head.

"I know what to do," Gunner said. "I'll nail him. Do whatever it takes."

"Weren't you listening?" Colt fired back. "That's not how we play. That's not how we ever should have played."

"Says who?"

"Says me! I'm Coach now."

Colt knew Gunner would do anything to make his dad proud. The same way Colt wanted to make his dad proud. But there was no time left to argue. He had to trust Gunner to make a clean hit. He ran onto the field and held his breath.

The referee blew his whistle to start the play. Travis took the snap and stepped back into the pocket. His eyes darted left and right looking for an open receiver in the end zone. Colt and Bulldog charged over the line, but were blocked by the Hurricanes' big linemen. Colt was going nowhere. All he could do was watch.

He saw Gunner blast from the line. His eyes burned red like he was possessed by the devil. He ran straight for the quarterback. It didn't look like anyone could stop him. Gunner had his head down. He had Travis Valiant in his crosshairs. Then it happened. One of the hulking linemen raced from the other side. He was like a runaway truck without brakes. Gunner never saw him coming. The lineman's big shoulder pads smashed against his helmet. Gunner fell to the ground. And stayed there. He didn't move.

Travis found an open receiver. He fired a pass into the end zone. His wide receiver hauled it in. The Hurricanes had scored again.

Colt and Bulldog didn't even see the touchdown though. They had rushed to Gunner's side the second he'd been hit.

"Are you okay?" Colt asked, kneeling.

"I never saw him," Gunner groaned. "Did they score?"

Colt nodded.

"It's my fault."

"No, you got blindsided," Bulldog said.

"Yeah, I got popped pretty good. I'm a little woozy."

Colt and Bulldog helped their teammate up.

"Let's get you to the sideline," Colt said. He put Gunner's arm over his shoulder and they trudged off the field.

A minute later the whistle blew, sending the two teams to their benches for halftime. Colt glanced up. The Warriors were down 14–7. They were taking a hit on the scoreboard, and on the field.

20 HEADCASE

"Shake it off, Greg."

Sergeant Nelson's hands were on his hips. He looked down at Gunner, who was slumped on the bench. "When the second half starts I expect to see you out there."

"He got hit on the head, Mr. Nelson," Colt said. "He's a bit groggy."

"It's nothing. He's been hit before," Sergeant Nelson said. "You can play through it, Greg."

Colt studied Gunner. His shoulders were hunched. His arms hung limply by his side. His eyes looked glazed. Colt wasn't so sure he could play through it.

He wasn't the only one.

"I've seen that look before," Andrea said. She took a photo of Gunner and slung her camera over her shoulder. "It's the same look Tyrone Hill had when they carried him off."

Sergeant Nelson gritted his teeth. "You don't know Greg. He's tough."

"I know he is," Colt said. "But he got his bell rung. He's not himself."

Sergeant Nelson pointed at his son. "This is the biggest game of your life, Greg. You've got to get back out there."

Gunner tried to stand up. His legs wobbled before he slumped back down.

Colt had to make a decision. Should he let Gunner play like his father wanted? Or keep him on the bench? He wondered what Coach would do.

A week ago Coach would have sent Gunner back out there. All he'd cared about was winning. But his dad wouldn't do that now. He'd learned what a hit to the head could do. How it could make people do things they might regret for a long time. And how it could hurt the people they cared about most.

Colt had made up his mind. He spoke firmly. "Gunner, you're staying on the bench for the second half."

Sergeant Nelson's face turned blood red. "I didn't come here just to see my boy sit on the bench. Who are you to say he can't play, anyway?"

"I'm the coach."

"How can you be the coach? You're just a kid."

Colt looked Gunner in the eye. "Remember what happened to Tyrone Hill?"

Gunner nodded slowly and winced.

"Well, I don't want that happening to you. You can't play until you're checked out by a doctor. And that's not happening today."

Gunner looked up at his father. "It's over, Dad. I can't do it. I can't even walk. I'm sorry I let you down."

Sergeant Nelson narrowed his eyes at Gunner and shook his head. "I expected more from you, Greg." Then he turned and walked away.

Colt felt bad for Gunner. There was a time when his dad would have done the same thing. When he would have cared more about playing through the pain and winning, than about his own son. But Coach had changed. He hoped Gunner's dad would change, too.

The referee blew his whistle to start the second half.

Colt stood on the sideline giving Keegan last-minute instructions. The rest of the Warrior offence ran onto the field to receive the kick-off.

"I'm not used to such a loud crowd," the Warrior quarterback said.

Colt grabbed Keegan by the shoulder pads. "Just pretend they're the audience and you're about to go on stage. You've rehearsed a hundred times. You know the plays just like you know your lines."

Keegan strapped on his helmet and nodded. "The curtain's going up."

Colt pushed the tall quarterback onto the field. "You can do it, man. This game is ours."

Colt's pep talk worked. With Keegan calling the plays, the offence steamrolled down the field. The Hurricanes had no answer for the Warriors' bruising running attack.

Led by their powerful halfback, they pounded their way to a series of first downs. When the Hurricanes' defence was sure there'd be another run, Keegan would launch a pinpoint pass. Anthony hauled in his last throw and the speedy Warriors' flanker dashed into the end zone. The convert was kicked. The score was all tied up 14–14.

The second half see-sawed back and forth. Neither team was able to mount an attack. And then, with only two minutes left in the game, the Warriors were on the march. Two quick passing plays from Keegan moved the ball to the Hurricanes' forty-yard line. The Warriors were closing in for a score. A touchdown might win the game for them. Keegan called for a third pass in a row, but the Hurricanes wouldn't be fooled again. Their defensive backs waited for the ball like a pack of hungry jackals.

Keegan's throw floated over the middle on its way to their big tight-end. The Warriors' receiver looked like he was open, but the Hurricanes' safety had read the play a mile away. He picked the pigskin out of the air, tucked it under his arm, and took off down the field. He galloped all the way to the Warriors' ten-yard line before he was tackled.

The Warriors' defence trudged onto the field for the last time. There were just twelve seconds left. This was the final play. Colt raised his arm and called for a huddle. Bulldog, Jamal, Sanjay, and the rest of the team gathered around him.

"This is it, boys," Colt said, fiercely. "We have to stop the quarterback before he can make a play. And we have to do it without Gunner."

"I've got nothing left," Bulldog said. "My legs are beat."

"Their receivers are too fast for us," Sanjay said, shaking his head.

Colt knew it was up to him. He was the captain and the coach.

"I'll handle it."

He lined up across from the four hulking Hurricane linemen. He locked eyes with the quarterback who crouched behind them, calling the signals. Travis took the snap and backpedalled into the pocket. He was going to pass! Colt charged across the line knowing he had to bring him down before he could throw.

Colt rammed into the giant Hurricane player who blocked his path. He was the biggest player on the field. A human wrecking ball who must have weighed 220 pounds. The Hurricane knocked Colt down like a bowling pin. But Colt bounced back up. He kept driving forward. Nothing could stop him.

Colt's legs churned. His arms pumped. Using every last ounce of energy he had, he lowered his shoulder at the quarterback's thighs. The hit was a lightning bolt. A thunderous crash like he was in the gauntlet. Colt had tackled the quarterback. But it wasn't in time. As Travis fell backwards he was still able to throw the ball. It was a desperation pass. The pigskin wobbled through the air towards the end zone.

Colt looked up from the ground. He could see Sanjay was waiting to intercept the ball. That would save the game. But then he saw another player in a red Hurricanes' uniform flying across the field. The receiver leaped into the air and reached out his arms. Like a miracle, the ball landed on his outstretched fingertips. He pulled the leather into his chest and squeezed tight as he fell to the ground. The referee raced to his side to make sure he held on. Then he raised both arms straight up. Touchdown!

The Hurricanes had scored on the last play. They had won the game. The rest of their team poured onto the turf to share the 21–14 victory. The Hurricane fans flooded after them. The field was a sea of red.

All the attention was on the winning team. Almost no one noticed the fallen Warrior still on the field.

"That was the greatest tackle I've ever seen," Bulldog said, reaching down a hand.

"You could have gone headhunting," Jamal said. "You could have speared him and stopped the touchdown."

"But you didn't," Sanjay said.

Bulldog pulled up his friend. "You hit him clean."

Colt's body was battered and bruised. He had sacrificed for the team. He'd played the way he always wanted to play. He hadn't been able to bring the Warriors to victory. But he had brought them something more. Pride.

21 THE LAST STAGE

The gym was packed. Principal Holly had called a special assembly. Attendance was mandatory for every Woodside student.

Colt stood backstage with Bulldog, Gunner, and the rest of the team. The players had slipped on their Warrior jerseys and waited hidden from view. He had never been behind the curtain peering out into the crowd before. Not like Keegan.

"Hey, Romeo!" Bulldog kidded the quarterback. "Where are your red tights, bro?"

Principal Holly stepped up to the black microphone that stood in the middle of the stage. Some of the kids in the audience clapped while some whistled. Colt even heard a few boos. *Being a principal must be a tough job,* he thought.

"Welcome, everyone," the principal said. Her voice was loud and echoed through the gym. "It's not very often you have a pep rally to celebrate the loss of a football game. But we are today, and for good reason."

Colt agreed. He recalled the exciting rally right here in the gym the day before the championship. Everyone got pumped up. There had been speeches, music from the school band, and the cheerleaders had made up a special song:

Hurricanes, Hurricanes, blow, blow, blow!
Warriors, Warriors, go, go, go!

Colt couldn't ever remember Woodside having a rally after a game, though.

"The first order of business is to bring out your Warriors' football team!" Principal Holly waved at Colt to come onstage. He led the players across the stage where they formed a long line. The crowd went crazy, cheering wildly.

The principal addressed the audience in a more serious tone. "The last two weeks have been like a rollercoaster ride for the Warriors. First, they were up by winning the semi-final game against the Pembina Panthers. Then they were down when a Panther player was seriously hurt and the co-captain of our team was suspended. It was a tough time for all the players. But even more so for one in particular — Colt Taylor."

The crowd broke into applause and wouldn't stop. Colt could feel goosebumps on his arms. He scanned the gym and saw one girl clapping a little harder than the rest. Andrea smiled up at him from her seat in the front row. Colt felt relieved that people knew the hit on Tyrone Hill wasn't his fault. But he was embarrassed by all the attention. He raised both hands asking the crowd to quiet down.

"Now, Mrs. Drago would like to say a few words to Colt."

Colt watched the Dragon Lady fly across the stage with her green dress flapping behind her like wings. He hadn't handed in his book report yet and worried that she might ask him why it was late in front of the whole school.

The Dragon Lady swept a hand over her spiky, red hair. "I know it's hard to believe, but sometimes we teachers make mistakes."

"All the time!" a boy in the audience shouted.

The crowd exploded in laughter. Mrs. Drago glared into the sea of student faces before speaking again.

"I just want to personally apologize to Colt for judging him before I had all the facts. He's not the dirty player I thought he was but a fine, upstanding young man." Mrs. Drago turned and smiled at Colt. "Now, if he just handed in his homework on time he'd be a perfect student as well."

The Dragon Lady swooped off stage to more laughter and a few cheers. Principal Holly swooped back on. "The Warriors played their hearts out yesterday even though they didn't have Coach Taylor. I asked Coach to say a few words today, but he said he wouldn't be attending the rally. He said he didn't want to take any attention away from the players."

Colt knew this was true. He wished everyone knew how sorry his dad was for the suspension he had received right before the big game.

Principal Holly looked out over the crowd. "I don't know exactly what Coach Taylor would have said, but I'm sure he would have sent his congratulations to the team."

"I know what he'd say."

The principal spun around to face the long line of players that stretched across the stage. "Who said that?"

"I did," Colt said, stepping forward.

"Would you like to speak for Coach Taylor?"

Colt nodded and walked to the microphone. He gazed at the crowd of students that was packed into every corner. He wondered what they were thinking. Would they cheer or boo? The room fell silent.

Colt started slowly. "What would Coach Taylor say? What would my dad say? He'd say he shouldn't have coached yesterday's game. That he didn't deserve to. That he knows what he did was wrong. And that he's vowed to never let that happen again. He'd tell you that he watched the game just like you. And he'd tell you what he told me. That he saw a team play with more guts, more determination, and more heart than any he's ever coached."

Colt looked over his shoulder. The players were hanging on every word just like they were in the locker room.

"But what made Coach the most proud was that the team played fairly. They showed their school, their teammates, and themselves that you don't have to win to hold your head high." Colt looked out over the sea of faces one last time. "That's what Coach would say."

He didn't know how the crowd would react. But at least now they would know what kind of man Coach really was. The kind of man he was before all the headaches, all the forgetting, and all the outbursts. The kind of man they could all look up to.

Colt didn't have to wait long. After his final words there was no doubt how the audience would respond. A wave of pride swept across the gym. Every student and teacher stood and cheered.

As the crowd rose to its feet, Colt raised his hand.

"Let's bring it in!" he called.

Bulldog, Gunner, Keegan, Sanjay, Jamal, and the rest of the players rushed forward and huddled around Colt. One last huddle for the team. One last huddle for the season. One last huddle for Coach.

Colt thrust his fist in the middle of the circle. The team did the same.

"Warriors!" he shouted.

"Warriors!" the players shouted.

"Warriors!" the crowd shouted.

THE LOWDOWN ON
CONCUSSIONS

Concussions are common in sports, especially contact sports like football.

What exactly are concussions?

Concussions are brain injuries. Normally, the brain is cushioned from everyday bumps by the fluid that surrounds it. But sudden, strong movement can cause the brain to slide against the inner walls of the skull. Concussions can result.

You do not need to be knocked out to get a concussion. Any blow to the head, face or neck — or even a hit to the body that shakes the head — could cause a concussion.

Because concussions can happen in different ways, sometimes it is difficult to know when someone has one.

Here are some common symptoms and signs of a concussion:

+ **Thinking Problems** — general confusion (e.g. not knowing time, date, place, name of opposing team)
+ **Physical Symptoms** — headache, dizziness, nausea, stomach pain, feeling dazed, seeing flashing lights, ringing in the ears, sleepiness, double/blurry vision or a loss of vision, poor balance
+ **Behavioural Symptoms** — being slow to answer questions or follow directions, being easily distracted, poor concentration, inappropriate emotions or emotional response (e.g. laughing, crying or getting mad easily)

Concussions are serious. For the most part, the symptoms are temporary and people recover fully. But sometimes the symptoms of a concussion can last for years.

What should you do if you think a player has a concussion?

The player should be taken out of the game right away, and his or her parents or guardians should be told. Even if the symptoms go away quickly, the player cannot return to play until being examined by a doctor.

Learn more by visiting Parachute, a national organization dedicated to preventing injuries and saving lives, at http://horizon.parachutecanada.org/en/?s=concussion.

CHECK OUT THESE OTHER FOOTBALL STORIES FROM LORIMER'S SPORTS STORIES SERIES:

Red Zone Rivals
by Eric Howling

Quinn Brown has to prove to a new coach that he deserves to remain the Spartans' starting quarterback. But Coach Miller's style seems to be throwing Quinn off his game — and big-mouthed second-string Luke is gunning for Quinn's position. To top it off, Quinn has been paired up with a peer tutor for math, and the tutor's a new kid everyone's making fun of. Who would have thought that the new kid would be exactly the kind of friend a struggling quarterback needs — both on and off the football field?

Replay
by Steven Sandor

Growing up above his parents' Chinese family restaurant in Sexsmith, Alberta, Warren Chen has always dreamed of being a football star. At 90 pounds and five feet tall, he's not exactly built like a linebacker, but he is small, slippery, and no one can catch him. In their first game of the season, Warren reaches the end zone to score the game-winning touchdown — almost. But Warren celebrates anyway, and the referee buys it. Warren has to decide whether to come clean and cost his school the victory, or continue living the smalltown football dream.

LORIMER